The
Hustle
Chronicles
2

GAGED JUSTICE

BLACCSTARR
MEDIA GROUP

The Hustle Chronicles 2®

The Hustle Chronicles 2

Is a work of fiction. Any resemblances to real people living or dead, actual events, establishments, organizations, or locales are intended to give the fiction a sense of reality and authenticity. Other names, characters, places and incidents are either products of the author's imagination or are used fictitiously. Those fictionalized events & incidents that involve real persons did not occur and/or may be set in the future.

Published by:
BlaccStarr Media Group
Written by: BlaccTopp
Inside Layout: Linda Williams
Edited by: Dolly Lopez/Linda Williams
Cover design by: www.mariondesigns.com

For information contact:

BlaccStarr Media Group
P.O. Box 9451
Port St. Lucie, FL 34985-9451

blaccstarrmg@gmail.com
www.facebook.com/mrblacctopp
twitter...@mrblacctopp
instagram...@mrblacctopp
website: www.novelistblacctopp.com

Dedication

This book is dedicated to the ones whom I have lost, that were near and dear to me: Najé Brashford, my beautiful mother; my daddy, Rufus Swift Jr.; my two sisters, Reba Victoria and Anna Catherine; my Uncle Rabbit; and my stepdad, Mervie "Booty" Green. R.I.P. each of you. I miss you more than you will ever know. See you at the Crossroads!

Always,
Mr. BlaccTopp

Acknowledgements

First and foremost, I would like to thank the Almighty for all of the blessings that He has bestowed upon me.

I would like to thank my father (R.I.P.) for my tenacity and drive.

I would like to thank my mother, Najé (R.I.P.) for my artistic nature and my educational fortitude.

I want to say thank you to my editors, Linda Williams and Dolly Lopez. We are just beginning, ladies!

To my family at Black and Nobel Book Store, Hakim Hopkins and Tyson Gravity, thank you brothers sincerely!

To Treasure Blue; you have been a constant source of help and inspiration and I just want to say thank you. WRITE ON!

To Kalil, my only son, Kalani, my little "Noodle Booty" and my last pea out of the pod, Kailyse; my life belongs to you three, no questions asked. I love you with every ounce of breath in my body.

To all of you that I consider my friends, I thank you.

To the readers, thank you for allowing me to share my pain, my misery, my fantasies and my dreams. Without you I could not continue to do this.

*P*rologue

Not My Child

Naje' couldn't believe her eyes. *No, no, no!* she thought. *This can't be happening; not to my baby boy!* She and Devon rose at the same time and tried to weave their way through the aisles to get to the stage.

Devon knew it. He had felt it, and his gut was never wrong when it came to police. They reached the stage just as Detective Sweeney was leading Julius off of the stage. "Say man, where are you taking my little brother? What is he being charged with?" Devon asked nervously.

"This young man is wanted in connection with the murder of Irving Green. And who are you, if I may ask, son?" Sweeney asked incredulously.

"First of all, I'm not your son. And second, I'm Devon Gage, Julius' older brother," Devon shot back.

Just what we need! Another god damned Gage! Sweeney thought. He had done a thorough investigation of the Gages, and his findings didn't include a second son. Nevertheless, he wouldn't let it deter his plans. Yellow Shoes and Rabbit would have to pay extra for the second Gage. There were other Gage brothers, but from Sweeney's knowledge, they weren't into the fast life like Julius Sr. and Charlie Boy, so there was nothing to worry about coming from their end. Julius Sr.'s sons, however, were a different matter altogether. If Julius Jr. was as dangerous as the streets said he was, and he and his brother, Devon had linked up, then he was probably equally as dangerous. He would have to do some investigating into this Devon Gage.

"I'm Julius' mother, and there is no way my son committed any murder. He's a good boy. Do I believe he's an angel? No, but I don't believe he's capable of murder. You need to release him this instant!" Naje' demanded. She was beside herself with grief.

Angelica walked up with Mrs. Gray, trying to get some idea of what was going on.

Julius looked at Angelica lovingly. He hated for her to worry, but he knew that he was innocent of the charges. He had nothing to do with Booty Green's murder and he believed that things would work themselves out. "Jelly, baby, don't worry yourself. Remember the list that I gave you?" he asked.

"Yes, baby, I remember. Why?"

"Get with my brother and call the very first number on that list. I love you, Mama. I'll be okay. No need to worry. They can't hold me."

Chapter 1

I'm All In

Julius was livid. How could he be sitting in jail on his graduation day? He wasn't worried because he knew he hadn't killed Booty Green. Nevertheless, the Dallas Police were known for planting evidence to make a case stick. But it didn't matter, because as soon as Angelica made that phone call he would walk. Julius had a full army of attorneys at his disposal courtesy of Mr. Barrera.

He lay back on the bunk and thought about his situation, and chalked it up as karma. He was nobody's angel and he had put in a lot of work in his short eighteen years, so it was only natural for things to catch up with him sooner or later. He couldn't think straight and his mind was clouded.

The detective told him in not so uncertain terms that he was being set up by Rabbit and Yellow Shoes. It was all coming together for him now. They wanted to frame him for Booty Green's murder to cover their own asses. They knew that Julius was dangerous and probably felt as though Booty Green was in too deep. Yellow Shoes was a coward in Julius' book. *He should've just come to me like a G,* he thought.

Then his mind shifted to his mother. If Yellow Shoes and Rabbit were eliminating everyone that could implicate them in the murder, then it wouldn't be long before they went after Naje'. He needed to see Angelica and Devon.

"Hey, CO!" Julius yelled. "Hey, CO!" he screamed louder.

"Stop yelling, son. What do you need?"

"Man, I need to use the phone."

"This ain't your first rodeo. You know you have to wait until you get upstairs."

"I know that, man, but my mama might be in danger!" the young man said desperately.

The old man looked at the kid who was still in his purple cap and gown with a golden sash. There was something in his eyes that made the elderly man believe the story. The boy looked shaken and rattled, as though he had made some sort of startling discovery. "Alright, son, I'ma let you use the phone, but you gotta make it quick. I'll give you five minutes."

"That's all the time that I need, sir. Thank you," Julius said politely. He didn't notice his hand trembling, but it was shaking almost violently.

Naje' answered the phone, and Julius could instantly tell she had been crying. "Hello," she said between sobs.

"Hey, Ma, are you alright? It's Ju."

"Hey, baby. No, I'm not alright, and I won't be until you're home. I'm waiting on Angelica to get here, and then we're coming to get you out," Najé replied.

"Where's Devon, Mama?"

"He's right here, honey. Do you want to speak to him?"

"Yeah, but hold on. I want you to be really careful on your way here, Ma. Don't trust anybody but Jelly and Devon."

Naje' nodded as if Julius could see her agreeing through the phone. She then handed the phone to Devon.

"Hey, little bro. How are you holding up down there?" Devon greeted.

"I'm straight. Listen, I don't have much time," Julius said anxiously. "I need you to come down here with Mama and Jelly. There're some things that you need to know, and that I need you to take care of."

"Okay, man. Anything you say. I don't like jail houses, but I'll be there," Devon assured him.

"And Devon?"

"Yeah, bro?"

"Be careful, dog. There're some people that might try and hurt Mama, bro."

Julius replaced the receiver and thanked the old guard. He was confident that his family would take care of business, but they needed to hurry. The longer he sat in jail, the more likely it was that the corrupt detectives would have the time to solidify their bogus case.

His thoughts shifted from worry to happiness, and back to worry again. God forbid they hurt Angelica; it was no longer all about his life. Angelica was pregnant with his child and he held their happiness in the palm of his hand.

Julius paced the small holding cell, wanting to scream. He felt helpless, and it was an unsettling feeling.

"Gage, you have an attorney visit," The elderly CO said.

This was the visit that Julius had been waiting for. Hopefully the lawyer had some good news. He needed to touch the streets and do some major damage control.

He was led down a narrow, dimly lit hallway to an even more dimly lit room. The attorney stood as Julius entered. They both waited until the guard left the room and closed the door. Julius smiled weakly. He remembered the lawyer from his meeting at Mr. Barrera's home.

"Mr. Gage, we have a lot to discuss and very little time to do it," the man said, very businesslike.

"I'm all ears, sir. This case is bullshit—no disrespect intended. I didn't like the man, but I didn't kill him."

"We are well aware of that. Mr. Barrera and his family are working hard to change the events that have occurred in the past weeks. There is no need for you to worry; you should be out of here within hours."

Those were the words that Julius had been waiting to hear. "So, what is the procedure now?" he asked.

"Mr. Barrera has sent someone to post your bond. Once that's finalized, we only have to wait until it's processed. It usually takes anywhere from a half hour to two hours. So at worst, you're looking at a maximum of two hours before you're released," the man said as he rose to leave. He extended his hand to Julius and added, "Mr. Barrera expects you at the mansion soon after your release, Mr. Gage." And with that he exited the small conference room.

As Julius stood to leave, the guard opened the door and ushered Naje', Angelica and Devon into the room. Angelica and Naje' were both crying, and it made Julius sad himself. The last thing that he wanted to do was to upset the two most important women in his life. "What are you gorgeous ladies crying for?" he asked, trying to lighten the mood.

Naje' hugged her son. She knew that he was afraid. It was written all over his face. She searched his eyes for any sign of bad news. If there was any, he wasn't showing it.

"Alright, this is the deal. I just had a meeting with the attorney before y'all came, and he says I should be out in a couple of hours. So now it's just a waiting game," he said in an attempt to reassure his family. "My main objective is to keep you guys safe from any and everything out there," he added.

"Safe from what?" Angelica asked.

"Safe from the men who killed my family, and my mother's husband."

Devon looked at Julius in disbelief. They had done a lot of talking, but his little brother hadn't told him that he knew who killed their father.

There was a thick tension in the room and the silence was deafening.

"I need for you two ladies to let me speak with my brother in private, please," Julius said.

Angelica and Naje' both started to protest, but Julius silenced them with the wave of his hand. Naje' smiled. He was so much like his father that it was ridiculous. She touched his face tenderly as she left the room with Angelica.

"I know you're probably wondering what the hell is going on, Dev man, and I'll explain everything to you when they release me. I don't want to talk in here. Walls have ears, you know what I mean?" Julius asked.

"Yeah, little playa, I hear you. So you're telling me that you know who killed Daddy n'em?"

"Yeah, I do. Just take Mama and Jelly out for dinner or something, and be back here in a couple of hours. I should be outside in front waiting for you by then. Don't let Mama drive. She drives badly when she's upset," Julius said with a laugh. Both men laughed at the thought.

"You have my word, bro. I'll protect them with my life."

The two men hugged, and Devon left the room.

Julius sat in a chair facing the door for a few minutes. He put his head down into his hands and took a deep breath. He had some devious visions milling around in his head. He wanted them to suffer. They would die one by one, but there wouldn't be any drive-by or cowardly hiding while he put in work. No sir, he was going in head first. It was what it was. If it was war they wanted, then it was war they were going to get. He would start with the weakest and end with the strongest and most annoying to send a definite message. He had missed the opportunity to exact his revenge on the man that was part of his families' execution. There would be no more mistakes and no more missed chances. Yellow Shoes, Rabbit and the crooked detectives would pay for their treachery.

Chapter 2

My Life, My Loss

Detectives Sweeney and McVey pulled into the driveway of Yellow Shoes' house. They had pressing business to discuss. The men exited the car and slammed both doors with force as if to announce their arrival.

Yellow Shoes stepped outside in a yellow silk robe and yellow slippers. Sweeney shook his head, thinking that the man was taking his *Yellow* Shoes persona too far.

"How may I help you fine gentlemen on this wonderful night?" Yellow Shoes asked sarcastically.

"I don't know why you're so goddamned chipper, because we have a major problem," Sweeney spat.

Yellow Shoes smiled. "Come in. Come in. Let's talk

about it. Don't panic. Everything is everything."

The detectives entered the house and looked around. They couldn't believe the sheer magnitude of the man's ego. His home was a genuine reflection of himself. Huge self-portraits were hanging from just about every wall that they saw.

The men were led through the house and out into the courtyard. It was surprisingly well kept, with benches made of brushed concrete and overly stuffed cushions arranged in a semi-circle. The benches faced a fire pit that burned brightly in the darkened atmosphere. Orange and yellow flames danced rhythmically as wooden embers crackled menacingly. The setting was appropriate for either romance or treachery; the latter being more befitting of the situation.

A petite Asian girl dressed in a short red and gold silk kimono appeared from nowhere as if beckoned by her pimp. She was jaw droppingly gorgeous. She was a spritely five feet tall, but her stiletto heels gave her an extra six inches. Her slender face housed a set of jade green eyes framed in a halo of jet black hair. Her olive skin glowed magnificently against the night fire.

It was always particularly interesting to McVey to see young beautiful women that were willing to allow themselves to be pimped and pandered by men that cared more about dollar signs than the well-being of these gorgeous vixens.

"May I interest you gentlemen in a beverage?" the

girl asked.

"No thank you, my dear. We're on duty," McVey said.

"Speak for yourself. I'll take a scotch on the rocks," Sweeney said.

"As you wish, sir. And for you, Daddy?" she asked, turning to Yellow Shoes.

"Nothing for me, Yummi. Daddy's fine, baby. But you can bring my friends and me fresh cigars, please," he said, dismissing the young Asian cutie. "These cigars are the finest Cubans money can buy. The taste is like a slice of heaven. Enough of that though. What is this urgent matter?"

"We have problems, Shoes. Not only did Julius make bond, but he has a brother — another Gage son. Did you know that?" Sweeney said nervously.

"And you're worried because?" Yellow Shoes asked, letting the question linger. "I mean I hate to sound cocky, but I'm not worried about some little teenage punks," he added. But in all actuality, he was terrified. His heart dropped into his stomach. It wouldn't be long before young Julius found out that he was responsible for this whole ordeal. Introduce another brother into the mix, and it doubled his danger.

"We can take care of both brothers, but it's going to cost you!" Sweeney screamed.

"First of all, lower you fucking voice, Sweeney! You work for *me*, honky; not the other way around. I will give you more money, but let's not lose sight of who is running shit. I have facilitated a very comfortable lifestyle for your alcoholic ass, and I will not be disrespected in my own home!" Yellow Shoes scolded.

As if on cue, Rabbit entered the courtyard carrying a glass of VSOP. He was followed closely by the young Asian girl carrying a silver tray with cigars and drinks.

"Yummi, these men are taking their drinks and cigars to go," Yellow Shoes said, as if dismissing the men.

"Yellow Shoes, what's going on, baby boy?" Rabbit asked with concern showing on his face.

"Slow motion, playa. These gentlemen were just leaving. Then we have some 'Musketeer' business to discuss," Shoes said to his old friend.

Rabbit got nervous immediately, Musketeer business was what Yellow Shoes referred to when he was talking about the Gages, and with Booty Green out of the picture there had to be major problems.

As if finally taking the hint, Sweeney downed his drink in one sloppy gulp, tapped his partner on the shoulder, and the two detectives left the home through the back gate leading to the driveway. Sweeny didn't like black people as it was, but he especially hated black people with money. Yellow Shoes was untouchable to him. They had been involved in so much criminal activity together that he knew without a doubt that Yellow Shoes could bury him and ruin his career.

Yellow Shoes looked at Rabbit, and although he was nervous himself, he didn't like the look on his friend's face. He looked shaken; like he was regretting everything that had transpired. Yellow Shoes hoped silently that the man wasn't backing out of the Musketeers, because he didn't want Rabbit to meet the same fate that Booty Green had met.

Rabbit was different. He wasn't a threat to Yellow Shoes' strength, so he didn't mind keeping the younger man around. Booty Green, however, had been a thorn in his side. He challenged Shoes' authority, so he had been *taken care of*.

"So, according to Sweeney, Julius had two sons. Not only is there Julius Jr., but another son. No need to worry though. They will be dealt with swiftly."

"What the fuck, bro? This shit is getting too deep, man. I — d"

"Hold up, playa!" Yellow Shoes said, stopping his friend short. "I know you ain't scared! Haven't I always taken care of your ass? Calm down. It's taken care of. They will be dealt with, and everything will be over and done with," he said as if to quell the man's fears.

Rabbit was visibly agitated. His hand shook uncontrollably as he downed his drink and rose to leave. "It's cool, Shoes. I trust you. If you say there are no worries, then there are no worries," he said, trying to sound convincing.

"You need to let Yummi suck your dick before you

leave. Maybe that'll calm your nerves," Yellow Shoes said with a laugh.

As if hearing her name, the pretty Oriental girl appeared with another Oriental girl named Jasmine in tow. "Please allow us to satisfy you, Mr. Rabbit. You will not regret it," Yummi said.

"That sounds out of sight, sweet baby!" Rabbit said with a sheepish smile. He disappeared into the house with the two olive skinned beauties, smiling like a child opening gifts on Christmas morning.

Yellow Shoes leaned back in his concrete captain's chair and lit his cigar. Rabbit would play his role and continue getting money, or he would die for free. The choice was his.

Chapter 3

You Owe Me

Julius walked out of the Dallas County Jail feeling surprisingly calm and exuberant.

Devon was out front waiting for him. He had dropped Naje' and Angelica off at home. Devon knew that Julius wanted him to stay with the ladies, but Naje' had insisted that they would be fine.

"What's up, jailbird?" Devon asked jokingly.

"Business, bro. Business. We have to go and meet with my supplier. That muhfucka is cool as shit, mane. He knew Daddy and shit," Julius said as he hugged his brother.

"A'ight, get in and let's ride. You're gonna hafta

17

tell me where to go. You know I don't know these Dallas streets."

"No doubt. Just jump on Stemmons Freeway and I'll tell you what exit to get off."

As the men drove the short distance from downtown Dallas to the Highland Park section of the city, Julius explained the entire situation to his brother; from the way their family was killed, to Booty Green marrying his mother. By the time Julius was finished explaining everything, Devon was furious.

"So, you mean to tell me that this shit has been going on this long and these sons of bitches won't let this shit go? Well, they got the right one this time, baby boy! It's on and cracking!" Devon said with anger clearly showing in his features.

"We have to be smart about shit, bro. I don't want anybody getting hurt, and I don't want anybody going to prison for these muhfuckas. Shit. They're already tryna frame me and shit, you know? Hey, take this Mockingbird exit."

The Barrera compound was unlike anything Devon had ever experienced. Even in the darkness he could see the extent of their wealth. When his little brother had told him that he was a gangbanging hustler, he envisioned him as a nickel and dime hustler working the corner, as so many young black men did. His brother, however, was on a whole different level. "Man, Highland Park is a world away from the Highland Park in Detroit," Devon said in amazement.

The armed guard at the gate recognized Julius, but he still followed protocol. "Mr. Barrera is expecting you. Mr. Julius. But whom may I ask is your friend?" he asked.

"This is my brother, Devon. I'm sure Mr. Barrera would be interested in meeting him," Julius responded.

Satisfied with the answer, the guard opened the gates.

"Man, you didn't tell me you were in this deep, bro. This is some gangster shit right here," Devon said.

The brothers were shown into the enormously plush mansion by a young Spanish girl. The home was so large that Devon could hear his footsteps echoing as they walked into the foyer.

Mr. Barrera greeted Julius with a firm handshake and a nod. Before he could introduce Devon as his brother, Mr. Barrera began to speak.

"Hello, Devon. Welcome to my home. We have much to discuss. Please, come into the parlor and have a drink with me," he said cordially.

"Excuse me, sir, but with all due respect, how do you know my name?" Devon asked.

"Young Gage, I am surprised that your brother hasn't explained to you that there is very little that I *don't* know."

Devon was both amused and amazed. He had been in business a long time in his chosen profession, and it was normally his job to know everything about everybody. This man was fast and proficient. Until a few weeks ago he didn't even know he had a brother, and here he was, standing in front of a man that knew who he was. *Shit, if he knows my name he probably knows a lot more than that*, he thought.

"Julius, it seems as though you have gotten yourself into quite a dilemma. These recent developments will pose a problem for our operations, so how do you suggest we handle it?" Mr. Barrera asked seriously.

"There's no need for you to worry, sir. I'll handle it. You have my word," Julius said.

"You have my full support and unlimited use of my resources at your disposal. If you or any of your boys need anything, please do not hesitate to call."

"This will be in-house, Mr. Barrera. The less people involved the better. I'm sure that between my brother and me we're more than equipped to handle the situation."

"Julius, I have no doubt in my mind that you and Devon are qualified to eliminate this threat. I suppose my main concern is that my family is insulated from prosecution. I trust that you understand my position?" the man said.

"Most certainly, Mr. Barrera. You have my word. Are we done, sir?" Julius asked.

"Actually no. There is more, my friend. Devon,

your penchant for taking a human life will serve you well within my organization. You may want to consider joining, as I have been known to take very good care of my people. I'm sure that your brother can elaborate more, young man," Mr. Barrera said, and walked out of the room.

It was actually eerie to Devon how someone could know so much about his business.

They left the Barrera estate in complete silence. Julius knew that his brother had questions, but now was not the time. He had to formulate a plan and quickly before someone on his side of the fence got hurt or worse.

"What are you thinking about, bro?" Devon asked as he drove towards South Dallas.

"I'm thinking about the best way to handle this situation. Rabbit will be easy because he's not built like that, you know? But the detectives and Yellow Shoes are going to be tricky. If we hit Yellow Shoes or Rabbit first, the detectives are going to get hip and use precautions, so we have to figure out the most productive way to do this," Julius told him.

"If you want my opinion, I say we start with the detectives, then Yellow Shoes, and end it with Rabbit. Rabbit should be last. We'll make the muhfucka sweat bullets," Devon said.

Julius glanced over at his brother. The darkness inside the car combined with the street lights was enough to cast a sinister shadow over Devon's face, revealing the murderous intent in his eyes. "Yeah, that sounds fine and dandy. But I want to do that punk ass Yellow Shoes last. I want him to *know* he's next," Julius said with a smile.

"Yeah, I'm with that. They thought that Daddy and Uncle Charlie Boy were raw? Wait until they fuck with us!" Devon said, and laughed loudly. His intentions were clear. He felt that Yellow Shoes and Rabbit owed him. They had taken his father far too soon, depriving him and his brother of their birthright. Devon usually killed for business, but these killings would be for pleasure.

Chapter 4

Shattered Promises

Mike Barrera paced back and forth in his office. He was furious. His nephew — his sister's son — had betrayed his family. There wasn't much that happened in the streets that Mike didn't know about.

Sleepy had crossed Julius, and it had been hastily brought to his attention. Mike didn't know how to deal with the situation. Any other time if a situation of this magnitude had presented itself to Mr. Barrera, the outcome was simple: betrayal and deceit were punishable by death and, Mike Barrera handled those offenses with swift ruthlessness.

But this situation was different. This was his blood,

and he cursed Sleepy for putting him in this awkward position. If he dealt with Sleepy the way that he was supposed to, his sister would hate him forever. On the other hand, if he let him get away with it, that would open up a floodgate of disrespect from all avenues.

Mike Barrera had survived years of street life by being smart, cunning and heartless. In the streets, love could often get you killed, and he wasn't dead yet.

Mike sat on the edge of his desk and stared out of his office window. It was just about dark outside, and the sunset painted the sky in a mixture of angelic shades of faint blues mixed with rustic oranges and golden yellows. It had been a while since Mike had actually noticed the beauty of his surroundings. He was blessed and very rich.

Mike Javier Barrera had come to this country like most other Mexicans. His mother had paid what meager earnings she had managed to save to have him smuggled into the United States when he was just a boy of nine years old. He had no blood relatives; only extended family that his mother had known since her childhood.

Mike had arrived in Texas with only the clothes on his back and a scrap of paper with an address scribbled on it. The address was to an old Mexican lady by the name of Miss Guerra. She was sweet to Mike, and she raised him as any loving grandmother would.

Miss Guerra had only one rule: Education was to be taken seriously and good grades were mandatory. As his adopted grandmother put it, "*Como extranjeros en este país ya tienen dos huelgas contra nosotros. Permitimos inteligencia eliminar una de esas huelgas.*" Simply put, "We, as Mexicans in this country already have two strikes against us. Allow intelligence to remove one of those strikes."

As a boy, Mike had worked very hard in school to make Miss Guerra proud. The United States had presented endless opportunities to the young Mexican, and he fully embraced them all. He flourished in his academics and he excelled in sports.

Mike's real motive was to create enough wealth to send for his mother, brother and sister. If he could save enough money to get them to the US, then his mission would be accomplished.

As a teen, Mike had taken any odd job that he could get, and he saved every penny that he had come across, except for the money that he gave to his *abuela*. She never asked for money, but he gave it freely. That was the least that he could do. She took really good care of him and never complained. She loved him and he loved her. His loyalty belonged to Miss Guerra. She only asked that he attend school, get good grades, and stay out of trouble. That wasn't hard to do at all, so Mike had taken on those tasks with enthusiasm.

When Mike turned seventeen years old, Miss Guerra had suddenly died in her sleep, and Mike was left alone in the big house in Laredo, Texas.

Soon after her death a lawyer had come to the

house and explained to him that Miss Guerra had never married and didn't have any children, so she had left her small fortune and her home to him in her will.

Mike couldn't believe his ears but, *Abuela* had taught him to never question a blessing. So, he simply paid his respects, bowed his head and gave thanks to God for sending him to Miss Guerra.

Without Miss Guerra he was lost, and the money made him vulnerable to the streets. He sold Miss Guerra's home and moved to Dallas. The thought of being in that big house without his *Abuela* hurt his heart, so to sell it didn't make him feel bad at all. His guilt was minimal, because he knew that his happiness was what she would want more than anything.

Once in Dallas, Mike sent for his mother, his brother and his baby sister. He had them brought over legitimately because he wanted his brother and sister to have all of the benefits that the US had to offer.

Dallas was a big city, and he noticed that although there were many Mexicans residing there, he was still looked upon as a "wetback". His education consisted of mostly book sense, but he wasn't exactly slow when it came to the streets.

Mike was a good listener and he always made sure to listen more than talk. The way he saw it, if you were talking then you couldn't be listening. So, he kept his head high and his mouth closed.

His little brother was sixteen years old when they'd

finally made it to Texas, and Mike couldn't have been happier. His sister was only six, and she was beautiful. Every time he looked at her his heart skipped a beat. She was truly his heart.

His little brother was a different story. He spoke broken English and had no desire to do any better. It was hard to explain to his brother why education in a country that was not their own was so important.

But Antonio Barrera wanted money, and he didn't want to work for it. He would tell his brother, Mike that he had allowed the Americans to make him soft.

Mike disagreed. He knew that he wasn't soft; he was smart. Mike was always thinking. At night when he tried to go to sleep it was next to impossible, because his mind was always racing.

His brother had plans of his own though. He had started school, and the young Mexicans at his high school were selling a lot of drugs. They came to school every day with big wads of money and nice cars. Antonio — or Flaco as his friends called him — wanted in.

Mike noticed an attitude change in his brother. He was dressing differently, his English was improving, and he wanted money, and lots of it.

Mike sat his younger brother down one day after school to pick his brain. "What's the deal, *mi hermano?*" he asked.

"Nothing, Mike. Why do you ask?" Antonio responded and shrugged.

Mike looked at his little brother closely. He knew that he was lying, but he had no way of knowing for sure.

"Okay, *mi hermano*, this is the deal. The *vatos* at school have a lot of money. They have the girls, they have the cars, and they get all of the attention..." Antonio paused to let the weight of his words sink in, and then continued. "You send me to school every day, and all day I sit in class wishing to be them. I—" before he could finish Mike interrupted.

"Jealousy is a fatal disease, little brother. It can lead to death."

Antonio waved his hands and sucked his teeth. "I am not jealous, Mike. I am intrigued. We could be getting money like those *vatos*. If you back me financially, I could make us rich," he said eagerly.

Mike had to admit that it was worth listening to. His little brother really knew a lot about drugs. But how he knew, Mike couldn't figure out.

As if sensing his brother's questions, Antonio stood up and grabbed both of his shoulders. "*Vato*, you always tell me to listen and not speak. The dudes at school love to talk. They don't think people are listening, but I am."

Mike was impressed. "And how much will this little venture set the Barrera brothers back, Antonio?" he inquired.

"I guess it depends on whether you want to start small, or go big, brother," Antonio countered.

"Well, you know everything is big in Texas, and if we're going to take a chance, let's take a big chance," said Mike.

And that was it. Just like that, Mike Barrera's younger brother had come to the states and introduced him to the street life. And, he had lived up to his word. They were rich beyond his wildest dreams. His days working at the tire shop on Gaston Avenue had been short, and he didn't mind it at all.

Today though, his worries weren't with the past; they were with the future. Family was family, but money was money, and his nephew was threatening his money in a huge way. If anything happened to Julius Jr., his money would suffer. They owned Dallas, and a large part of his success was because of Julius.

His nephew was treacherous and his actions had to be dealt with, but he had to figure out how to do it.

Antonio knocked lightly at his brother's office door.

"*Entrada!*" Mike said.

When Antonio entered, he knew that his brother was bothered, and it in turn bothered him. "What seems to be the problem, brother?" he asked.

"Have a seat, *mi hermano.* I must speak with you about this matter, because I am very confused."

Antonio knew it had to be serious. His brother was never confused and very seldom asked for his opinion.

Once Antonio was seated, Mike told his little

brother of their nephew's betrayal. He explained how much money they stood to lose if anything happened to young Julius. He explained his sense of confusion and his apparent hesitation.

Flaco thought for a long while, and then started speaking, choosing his words carefully. "My dear brother, you are a businessman. And although Sleepy is our only nephew, he must be dealt with. It's as you say: if you allow him to operate this way, we'll not only lose money, but the respect of the streets. A large part of our success lies in the relationships that we have forged with people over the years. We are a family of honor, and we have always been able to stand on our word. This level of deceit is dangerous, and it is something that we cannot allow, not now, not ever," Flaco explained.

Mike knew that his brother was right and he valued his opinion, but he loved his nephew. It was a very hard decision, and at the end of the day the decision was ultimately his alone.

He made up his mind. He would let the streets hold court on Sleepy. That way he could look his little sister in her eyes, knowing that her son's blood was not on his hands.

Chapter 5

The Shit Is Gonna Hit the Fan

As Julius and Devon drove towards South Dallas, they were both lost in their own thoughts.

Before they made it to Naje's house, Julius wanted Devon to meet his boys. He wanted his brother to incorporate himself into every aspect of the world he was a part of. He knew that Devon had his own world, but if they combined their two worlds, they would be rich beyond their wildest dreams. Julius was intelligent enough to realize that there was an immense amount of money to be made. "Instead of taking the Forest Avenue exit, go down to the Hatcher Street exit. I want to show you some shit," he instructed his older brother.

Devon simply nodded and kept driving. He wasn't trying to be short, but his mind was clouded. Committing murder had always come easy to the young Gage, but this was different. He was searching for a way to remove his emotions from the situation. Emotionally charged killings usually led to mistakes, and that wasn't a chance he wanted to take.

He steered the vehicle onto the off ramp of Hatcher Street. At the red light Julius instructed him to turn left. "Where are we headed bro?" he asked out of sheer curiosity.

"We're going down to my hood. I want you to meet my niggas, like I told you earlier."

The neighborhood that they entered was more of what Devon was used to. Litter was strewn about the streets, dope fiends and drug dealers were conducting open deals in plain sight, and the police presence was heavy, but no one seemed to give a damn.

There was a liquor store on just about every corner, not five hundred feet from it was either a school in one direction or a church in the other. Women went in and out of parked cars, turning tricks while their crack head boyfriends stood nearby sucking on the glass stemmed crack pipes waiting in the wings. The pungent, sweet, sickly odor of sizzling crack rock loomed heavily in the air.

Devon shook his head in disbelief. It never seemed to amaze him to what extent people were willing to go for a hit of that glass dick. He had seen mothers sell their children's Christmas toys *on* Christmas day. The gifts would be half wrapped, as if they had let the children unwrap them, look at them, and then off they went to the nearest dope-hole to swap products.

They turned onto Dixon Avenue, headed towards the Prince Hall Apartments.

"These two niggas I want to introduce you to are my OG's, man. I look up to these cats, bro. They always kept it real with me, you know?" Julius said proudly. He knew in the underworld there were very few loyal people that one could depend on. Duddy and D-Train had never let the young soldier down, no matter what the situation.

The Dallas Police Department's Gang Task Force Unit was doing their usual rabblerousing. The swirling lights of four police cruisers had a gang of YG's in the usual position; on their knees facing the wall, and ankles crossed with their fingers interlocked behind their heads. It was routine, so it wasn't even surprising to Julius anymore.

They pulled into Prince Hall, and Devon parked. Julius wondered if anyone would say anything about his brother having on a red T-shirt and red Chuck Taylor All-stars. Devon didn't gangbang, but there were a lot of BG's that would love to make a reputation for themselves by putting in work.

Julius dismissed the thought just as quickly as it

had come. His reputation was solid in his neighborhood, and they had to know that he wouldn't be caught dead with a Blood, let alone walk through the hood with one.

"Aye, nigga, you coming through the hood with slobs now, Ju?" one boy asked.

Julius shot the boy a menacing glance. The boy couldn't have been but thirteen or fourteen years old, but they were the most dangerous. "You know better than that, lil' homie. This is my brother. He don't gangbang, fool!" Julius shouted.

"Oh, okay. Make me know it then, cuzz," the young man said while putting his pistol back into the waistband of his jeans.

Julius shook his head and smiled. *At least the little fools are on point,* he thought to himself.

"These little niggas are for real about this gangbanging shit, huh?" Devon asked. "Kinda reminds me of the Disciples and Vice Lords up around my way," he added.

"This shit is serious around here, dog. Niggas be wildin' on the gang thing. I guess it doesn't help that the Blood neighborhood is literally like right across the tracks. We're always beefing with them slobs, bro. It's all about the money. People think we be into it because of colors. I mean, you choose your side, but we're beefing because of drug turf. The more area you control, the greater the money," Julius explained.

To Devon it sounded as if Julius was trying to

justify the gang wars. It was silly to Devon, but who was he to knock his little brother's hustle? If he liked it, Devon loved it.

They reached the door and knocked.

"Who is it?" asked the voice on the other side of the door.

"Aye, it's Ju, cuzz."

The door opened and a cloud of thick marijuana smoke came rushing out. "What it was, cuzz? Your Mom must have told you I called," Duddy said.

"No, cuzz. You tried to call me? What's up?" Julius asked. Duddy never called Najés house unless something was wrong. Julius couldn't think of any dilemma that would warrant Duddy calling him at home, but you could never tell with Duddy.

"Cuzz, remember the wetback you introduced me to? Sneaky I believe his name was?" Duddy asked.

"Naw, his name is Sleepy. Why? What happened?"

"Yeah. My nigga, that little bitch is treacherous. You know the streets love to talk, and word on the street is that Sleepy went to Yellow Shoes, Booty Green and Rabbit and told them that his uncle had told you that they were responsible for your family's murder. That's why you've been going through this bullshit, because he set this shit in motion, cuzz!" Duddy said.

Julius' blood ran cold. He was furious. He hadn't done anything but try to be respectful and nice to the young Mexican.

"You know the worst part about it though, homie?" Duddy continued.

Julius didn't believe that there could be a worse part, but whatever. "What's that?" he asked.

"He started all of this on some emotional shit. He was upset because he felt like his uncle was closer to you than to him. That's some real bitch shit right there, nigga."

Julius couldn't believe his ears. He had always given Sleepy his props. And worse still, he had even given the Mexican kid parts of his heists as a sort of tribute for turning him on to his uncle in the first place. "I'm going to deal with that muhfucka as soon as I see him, cuzz! That wetback fuckboy's gotta see me!" Julius said, his frustration and anger showing plainly.

"Well, you might get the chance sooner than you think," Duddy said, laughing.

"What's that supposed to mean, cuzz?" Julius asked.

Duddy nodded to a boy barely thirteen years old. The teen opened a door to the back bedroom to reveal Sleepy duct taped to a chair. He was badly beaten, and as he watched, D-Train and another young gangbanger named K-Lo beat him some more. With every swing of their brass knuckle-clad fists blood leapt from his swollen face.

Julius stepped into the room, and both men stepped aside. "Sleepy, why, homie?" he asked. "Why would you try to get me fucked off when all I did was attempt to be cool with you, dog? I helped you make a lot of money!" he said angrily.

Sleepy looked up and tried to focus through the layer of blood that covered his eyes. His head hurt and his mouth was dry. He wanted to speak, but he couldn't form his words. He knew that he was going to die and it frightened him to no end. He contemplated begging but he had done too much dirt to hope to be spared. He said a silent prayer to himself before trying to speak. "I... I...I..." he said, unable to get his words out clearly.

"Sleepy, you need to tell me something, man." Julius' anger was building. He looked at his brother, who was leaning in the doorway with his arms crossed and watching the spectacle.

"Ain't this old dude's nephew?" Devon asked.

"Yeah, it is. Why you ask?"

"It just stands to reason that he's going to feel some kind of way about y'all doing his nephew, that's all."

It hadn't actually crossed Julius' mind, but Devon was right. When Mr. Barrera was informed that Sleepy had been murdered, he would spare no expense in avenging the murder of his nephew. The shit was about to hit the fan, and Julius knew it.

"Listen, baby brother. I know that this shit is going to cause a war, but trust me when I tell you, even if you let him go right now, there will still be a problem," Devon said.

"I know, I know, but shit it is what it is," Julius said.

Devon saw a Glock 9mm pistol sitting on a nightstand across the room. He moved across the room casually, picked up the pistol and looked at it. He then grabbed a pillow from the bed and ripped the pillowcase off of it and wiped the gun clean of fingerprints. "If we're going to go to war with his family, we might as well give them a good reason," he said as he walked to the chair that Sleepy was taped to.

He grabbed a handful of the young Mexican's hair, pulled his head back and put the pistol into his mouth. "Make sure when you get to hell you tell Satan that I sent you, muhfucka! I got an account with him!"

Sleepy blinked, and one bloody tear dropped from his eye. He looked at Devon, unable to speak but silently pleading for his life with his eyes.

Devon looked deep into Sleepy's eyes and found what he was searching for; that slight twinkle—an ever so present hint of a soul that he was about to lose.

Devon smiled his wickedly straight white smile and pulled the trigger twice. Sleepy's head exploded as he slumped forward and slid into darkness.

Chapter 6

This Ain't What You Want, Playa

Shayla stepped off of the plane and surveyed her surroundings as she often had in the past. *Dallas must be a huge ass city with an airport this large,* she thought.

Devon had called her and told her that he needed her. At first she thought that he meant just for business, but he'd said, "That too." *That too? What did that shit mean?* "What do you mean, Devon?" she had asked him.

"I mean we fuck around from time to time but I want more. When my mom died I had a void in my soul, but slowly you've filled that void; not on no replacing my mom type shit, but you helped me feel again. I will never again in life find a woman that will do the things for me that you do, or make me feel the way that you make me feel. I guess what I'm trying to say is that I'm in love with you baby girl, and I never want to lose that. Listen, I'm going to relocate to Dallas, and if you feel the same way about me, you'll come join me," he told her.

And that was that. Shayla had gone to his condo, packed up all of his things, and then did the same at her apartment. She had gone to their weapons storage and put all of their guns into weapons crates. She then hired a moving company to move all of their belongings to Dallas. That had been two weeks ago. In Shayla's eyes that was plenty of time to find a place and have it ready.

Now she was there in Dallas, and she was starting her life over again, not only as his business partner but as his girl. This was new to her, and she liked it. In the past she had always felt that fucking him was just that; fucking him, even though she enjoyed it. Now they would be actively pursuing a life together.

She spotted Devon standing at the end of the long walkway leading from the plane to the terminal. She increased her pace to an almost trot. She ran up to him, threw her arms around his neck and kissed him deeply.

"What up, Pretty Black?" Devon asked her.

"What up, Gangster Red?" Shayla asked him, and blushed. She had been in love with Devon for a long time, and in every action from now on she wanted it to show.

"Damn, girl! It feels like I haven't seen you in like

forever!" Devon teased.

"Did you miss me, baby?"

"Damn skippy!" he replied.

"You just miss this wet gushy-gushy!" she said and laughed. She knew that it was more that. Devon had never really been good at discussing his feelings, so his wanting her there with him to start a life together told her all she needed to know.

"Yeah, you're right. I miss that yummy, but I really missed your presence. When you're not around I feel incomplete," Devon said.

"I know, baby. I was just bullshitting. I love this new side of you, Devon."

If there was anything that Devon loved about Shayla, it was her ability to be as gritty and raw as she wanted and needed to be, but still be a lady at the same time. He always felt as if he was with his best friend. The more he thought about it, the more he realized that she *was* his best friend. "I hope you like my little brother and his girlfriend, babe. They're cool as a muhfucka."

"I'm sure I will, baby, especially if he's anything like you."

Devon just smiled. He was anxious for Shayla to see how he was rolling. He'd recently purchased a new Mercedes Benz and gotten it in her favorite color. Shayla told him on more than one occasion that her dream car was a white on white Benz with a nice stereo system. He didn't understand why she hadn't bought one for herself because they had plenty of money. Nevertheless, it would be a nice surprise for his girl to start their new life together.

Devon saw an old beat up Chevy parked next to their car and seized it as an opportunity. He pulled the keys from his pocket and stepped to the trunk of the Chevy. The expression on Shayla's face was priceless. "What's wrong, baby girl?" he teased.

"Nothing, Daddy. It's just... I don't know. This is just an ugly ass car. It's not your style," she whined.

Devon tried to hold back his laughter as long as he could, until the look on her face was too much to bear. "Oh, so you're ashamed to ride in my ugly ass bucket, huh?"

"No, not ashamed. I love you so it doesn't matter. I'm just saying, why would you choose this car with as much paper as we have, baby?" she pouted.

He erupted into raucous laughter. He pushed the trunk button on his key chain and the trunk of the Mercedes sprang open.

Shayla's eyes lit up like an excited child as she playfully punched him. "Baby, you play too much!" she laughed. "I was going to buy you a car out of my own money!"

"You like it, sweets?" he asked.

"Yeah, I love it!"

"Good, because it's yours," he said as he tossed her the keys. "I've never been much for white cars." He added.

As he grabbed the luggage to load it into the trunk, Shayla gave him a bear hug from behind. "Thank you, Daddy! I love it, and I love you," she said.

Devon smiled to himself. He liked the softer side of her. They had conducted a lot of business together and had sex on a regular basis, but telling her how he felt had unleashed a side of her that she'd never let show before now.

They exited the airport parking garage and headed towards North Dallas. He wanted to introduce her to Angelica. With an impending war with the Mexicans looming, Jelly would need some support.

******

Julius had explained to Najé what had happened with Sleepy, and she reluctantly agreed to relocate to Miami only after Julius posed the question: "Do you want me to go back to prison or end up dead, Ma? Because if something happens to you, that's exactly what's going to happen."

Julius wanted her as far away from Dallas as possible so they had loaded her things into a U-Haul in the dead of night, put her car on a trailer and got on the road before the streets had an opportunity to wake up.

Julius and Devon had said their good-byes and flew back the next day. With Najé out of the picture, Julius had reassured his brother that he was ready for whatever came their way.

******

"Take the Valley View exit, Sweets," Devon said.

Minutes later they pulled into the gated community of Valley Crest. Devon got out of the car, walked around to the driver's side and punched in the five digit code— 00931—to open the gate. The gate squeaked to life and the pair wove their way through a tangle of winding roads.

They pulled into the driveway of a large two story red brick home that had security cameras mounted on each corner for additional safety. It was the typical suburban home, with the exception of the cameras.

A plush carpet of emerald green landscaping surrounded the home. Massive oak trees sat on each side of the dwelling as if to shade it from the brutally scorching Texas sun.

Shayla was in awe. When Devon said that he'd found a place, she had pictured a condo not unlike the one that he'd had in Detroit.

They went inside and were greeted with the soft sounds of Sade singing her sweet melodic tunes. It was dimly lit throughout the house except for slivers of sunlight peeking through the windows.

Devon called out to Julius and Angelica, but got no response. His skin started to tingle and the hair on the back of his neck stood up. He called out to his brother again, and this time Julius answered.

"Yeah, bro, we're out by the pool!" Julius shouted.

"Man, please don't scare me like that, dog! I thought the Mexicans got your ass!" Devon scolded.

"Yeah, I hear you. Jelly got the damn music up so loud that I couldn't hear you."

Angelica emerged from the pool. Her smooth young body glistened with the pool water. "Julius, the music isn't even that loud," she said.

Shayla was impressed. Julius and Angelica made a very handsome couple.

Devon studied his little brother. He looked so much like their father. Julius didn't seem to be worried about the war that was brewing, and if he was worried, he wasn't showing it.

"I want to introduce y'all to my Shayla," Devon said.

Shayla blushed. She was still trying to get used to being classified as his girlfriend.

"What's up, Shayla? Glad to have you here. This is my girl, Angelica, but we all call her Jelly," Julius said.

"Hey, girl, it's nice to meet you," Angelica said, giving Shayla a hug. "Don't mind Julius, child. He's special!" she added and laughed.

Julius playfully slapped her on her butt. "Special, huh?" he said.

They all laughed.

"Man, where's the herb at? Roll it up, bro. Stop holding out," Julius said jokingly.

Devon went inside the house and came back moments later with a gallon sized zip lock bag full of marijuana. They all took a seat at a table with a huge umbrella sheltering them from the sun. The pungent odor of the marijuana filled the back yard when he opened the bag.

Angelica got up from her seat and moved to a lounge chair out into the sun.

"What's wrong with Angelica?" Shayla asked.

"Ain't nothing wrong. She just doesn't dig the smell because she's pregnant," Julius told her.

"Aww, that's so sweet! Do you want a boy or a girl?"

Julius shrugged his shoulders "Shit, it doesn't matter to me as long as it's healthy."

Devon laughed at his little brother's veiled attempt at pacifying his lady. "Quit lying, fool. You know you want a boy."

"Whatever!" Julius responded and laughed. "Seriously, man, I haven't heard from Mr. Barrera since that shit with Sleepy happened. I don't know how I should take that shit, you know? I'm about to call him and find out what's going on," he said between puffs on the blunt.

"Fuck that shit! No news is good news, I always say. The way I look at it, when the time comes we should be ready. Fuck giving them head's up that we know there's a problem, you know what I mean?" Julius said angrily.

"Baby, honestly, I think we need to hit them hard and fast to send a message. Kill the head and the body will follow. Isn't that what you taught me?" Shayla added.

"Yeah, baby, that is what I taught you, but this is Julius' call."

"Damn, bro! I like her. She's about her business," Julius said.

"I'm just down for my man, and I'm extremely good at what I do. If it comes down to it, I'm ready to go to war. Fuck it!" she said.

Angelica looked at Shayla closely. She admired the young girl. Shayla was older than Angelica, but she looked young. Her sex appeal was evident, and Angelica couldn't help but notice that she had nice taste in clothes.

Angelica got up and went inside the house, and everyone else followed. "See, you guys are thinking like hoodlums. The Mexicans will be a problem, but if y'all handle it right, it can be done and our hands will be completely clean," she said.

"What do you mean by *our* hands? You're pregnant, so you need to be sitting back chillin', not worrying about this shit," Julius said to her.

"I don't have a choice but to worry. You're everything to me, and I'll be damned if I sit back and watch somebody hurt you. I may not be able to handle a gun like Shayla, but I can at least help with the planning," she said.

"I think Jelly has a point," Shayla chimed in. "If we go at them like they expect us to, they'll be ready. But if we go at them on some genius shit, they won't know what hit them."

Julius and Devon looked at each other. They had created monsters and they knew it.

"So, what do you ladies have in mind?" Devon asked.

By the obvious silence it was apparent that the plan hadn't been forged yet. The ladies just giggled.

Julius took that as a sign that they liked each other, and he was happy about that.

"Baby, I want to take Shayla to Valley View mall to do some shopping. May I have some money please?" Angelica asked.

Julius was about to go into his pocket to give Angelica some shopping money, when he was stopped short by Shayla who said, "It's okay, brother-in-law. I have money. Then she said to Angelica, "Girl, I got you. It's my gift to you and the baby."

Angelica was ecstatic. Growing up an only child was very lonely. She had no siblings and no cousins to play with. All she ever had was her mother, and it was too much at times. Having Shayla around would make things a lot more interesting.

Both women kissed their men as they left the house. Angelica wanted to spend some quality time with her newfound friend.

Once the girls left it was time to get down to business.

"Man, Angelica made a good ass point. If we go fucking with the Mexicans with guns blazing, we'll lose. They have more money and more guns," Devon said.

"Yeah, she did make a valid point, but we got more than just those bitch ass wetbacks to worry about, bro. Yellow Shoes and Rabbit are still out there. Those punk ass detectives are going to stay in our business until we either end up dead or in prison, and this Barrera situation needs to be addressed. The only thing that buys us time with the Barrera's is money. We make a lot of money with these dudes, so I'm thinking that's why we haven't heard from them. You want a drink or something, Dev?" Julius said. He went to a bar just off of the kitchen and poured himself a glass of Seagram's gin and orange juice.

"Yeah, just pour me a gin on the rocks, man. No juice."

"I guess my main concern is getting this shit over and done with, man. I mean, I'm going to be a daddy in six months so I ain't trying to get caught up. I still have this bullshit case hanging over my head, and my mama is way over in Florida, so this shit needs to end soon," Julius said.

Devon knew that his little brother was upset and frustrated. They were both silent for a very long time, and then Devon leapt to his feet. "I got it, bro! I got it!" he shouted.

"Well, spit it out, nigga!" Julius said and laughed.

"I'm still putting the shit together in my head, but if we can pull this shit off, my dude, we'll eliminate everybody in our way. Just give me until the morning to put my brain on it," Devon said.

"Okay, bro. I got some shit in my head too, so maybe we can put all these ideas together and form one major master plan," Julius said and shrugged.

The girls had been gone for hours, and Julius missed Jelly.

The doorbell rang and both men tensed up. Nobody knew that they lived out here, and Angelica had a key.

Devon took his pistol from his waistband and went to the door. "Who is it?" he asked sternly.

"It's us, baby. Open the door; our hands are full," Shayla said.

"Baby, we stopped by the grocery store after we left the mall. Can you and Devon grab that stuff out of the trunk, please?" Angelica asked.

Both men sprang into action, doing as they were asked.

After they finished, Devon grabbed Shayla and kissed her. "I missed you while you were gone, baby. I might hafta show you a little somethin'-somethin' later on," he said lustfully.

"It's funny you say that, because I bought a sexy little something at Victoria's Secret at the mall," she said and winked.

Angelica blushed. She wasn't accustomed to people being so open about their sexuality. She wasn't a prude, but there were certain things that she just didn't talk about in mixed company, partly because she felt it was inappropriate, and partly because she didn't have anybody to talk about it with. She and Julius didn't really talk about sex. Her man was more action than talking, and that wasn't a big deal to her.

Hearing Devon and Shayla talking like that made her horny. It stirred something deep inside of her. She loved Julius and he turned her on, but the pregnancy had her emotions and her hormones in an uproar.

Angelica didn't realize that she was staring at Julius until he began to speak. "You're looking at me like you need Big Daddy to put it on you!" he teased.

"I might need that, Big Daddy. I didn't buy a sexy teddy, but I think I can pull something out of my bag of tricks," she gushed.

"Yeah, well that's our cue, folks. I guess we'll see you guys in the morning," Julius said.

"Shit, Shayla! I thought we were freaky, baby, but my brother n'em got us beat!" Devon said.

The couples went their separate ways, each pair headed in separate directions.

The house was set up perfectly. There were two

bedrooms on each side of the house. Julius had chosen an upstairs bedroom on one side of the house, while Devon had chosen an upstairs room on the opposite side. The two downstairs rooms had been left empty, except for sparse furnishings for whatever guests the brothers happened to have.

Devon walked behind Shayla as she ascended the stairs. He was playfully pinching her butt with every step she took. He was happy with his decision to share his feelings with her. Most men would have thought that he was being soft, but he didn't give a damn. She was by far the realest female that he had ever met.

They hadn't always been involved with each other romantically. At one point it was all business, but now somehow he felt that their being involved would make their relationship, whether businesswise or romantic, just that much stronger.

Devon smacked Shayla on her firm, round butt and said, "Close your eyes, baby." He covered her eyes as they walked into the large bedroom.

While the girls were away at the mall, Devon had taken his time and spread rose petals all over the bed. Candle light danced and flickered from wall to wall, and the sounds of soft sexy music filled the room.

He uncovered Shayla's eyes, and she stood at the bedroom door in amazement. She dropped her shopping bags and gazed into the bedroom, dreamy eyed.

The room was huge. It was the size of her whole

apartment back in Detroit. The way Devon had the room set up was sexy to her, and it made her insides quiver. The bed was a California king sized bed with an overstuffed black satin down comforter. The comforter was pulled back to reveal red satin sheets. Next to the bed in a bucket of ice was a bottle of expensive champagne and a joint the size of a pinky and about the length of a pencil.

She turned to look at him, and something about the way he was watching her made her heart beat faster. Her whole body tingled as he turned her around to face him and kissed her soft, supple lips. He held her at arm's length, looked deeply into her eyes and said in a husky voice, "Look around, baby. This is the way that I want to treat you for the rest of my life."

She pulled herself closer to him, reached down and felt his arousal. "I'm going to shower, baby boy," she said as she took her clothes off and let them drop to the floor.

Devon watched as she walked away, heading towards the bathroom.

Shayla turned and looked back at him. Their gazes met as she asked lustfully, "You coming, babe?"

******

On the other side of the house in Julius and Angelica's bedroom, the couple sat on the edge of their bed. Angelica was crying, and Julius had no idea why.

"What's wrong, baby doll?" he asked.

"Honestly, I don't know, baby. My emotions are all jacked up, you know? I mean, I know you love me, but I feel so fat and unattractive!" she whined.

"Girl, you're trippin'. Number one, you're not even showing yet. And number two, even when you get as big as a house, I'ma still think you're sexy as hell," Julius said and kissed the tip of her nose. She smelled like strawberries and cream. It turned him on, and his nature started to rise. He loved the way Angelica looked when she was fresh out of the shower. Her hair was long and silky and had a slight curl to it when it was wet, and her skin had a glow about it.

Julius wondered how and why she felt unattractive, but it was his job to make her understand that she was still as gorgeous as the day he met her in third grade. "Baby, you are beautiful to me, and I'm sure there are a lot of men who wish they could have a woman as lovely as you. You're beautiful inside and out, Angelica. And you're sexy as fuck," he said as he lightly bumped her shoulder with his.

"You still think I'm sexy, baby?" she asked.

"Yeah, I do."

Angelica stood up and stood between Julius' legs. She took his face in her hands as she bent down and kissed his lips.

Julius caressed her hips, letting his hands glide to her soft round butt.

Angelica walked over to the stereo and pressed play on the cassette, as he watched her booty jiggle with each step. She had on yellow lace bikini panties and a yellow and white *Tweety Bird* wife beater. The sounds of Troop flooded the room with a sweet soulful sound:

> *"...All I do is think of you day and night.*
> *I can't get you off my mind.*
> *Think about you all the time, all the time..."*

Troop sang as she dimmed the lights to make love to the man of her dreams.

Chapter 7
Decisions Decisions

Mike Barrera had come a long way since his early years in the underworld. He had become more comfortable with his life of drugs and money. He had tried to keep his business separate from family, but he came to realize that the two were inseparable. The fact of the matter was that his business was a family business.

His sister had been distraught when they'd gotten the news about Sleepy. No matter how hard he tried he couldn't console her. She had frantically pointed out that what happened was his fault, and that he needed to fix it.

Barrera knew that his nephew had been killed in retaliation for Julius' situation, and it bothered him to no end. He and his brother had both decided to let the streets hold court on Sleepy, but not like this. There had been a brutality about the murder that didn't sit well with Barrera. Not only had Sleepy been shot in the face so that his family couldn't give him an open casket, but they had cut his tongue out of his head as if they were trying to send a clear message: *"Keep your mouth closed!"*

Mike Barrera sat behind his large desk and watched as his brother paced back and forth across the office floor. "What's on your mind, my dear brother?" he asked him.

"No puedo creer que vamos a dejar que este bastardo negro a llegar lejos con esto!" he spat.

Mike hated when his brother was angry. Everything he said was in Spanish. "In English, Flaco. This is an English speaking household," he said.

"I cannot believe that we are going to let this black bastard get away with this," he said more calmly.

"I am not *letting* him get away with anything. We have to handle this thing democratically. Julius Gage makes a lot of money for us, first of all. Secondly, although we have amassed an army of soldiers, Julius has men that are equally as dangerous and loyal to the young man. His brother is a hired killer for, God's sake." Mike said as he rose from his chair. "Things have gone far better than we could have ever hoped, Flaco. Do you know how long it would take to train another one of those young hustlers to do the things that Julius does?

The chemical mixture of cocaine and heroin is not an easy one to mix, let alone sell. And if I may remind you, my dear brother, he has been selling those speed balls by the kilo, which in turn bought that Lamborghini that you are so fond of!" Mike scolded.

"Yes, I know, *mi hermano*. It just pains me to know that our nephew has been so brutalized. He was not a good person inside, but he was still *familia*," Flaco said.

There were several ways that Mike Barrera could make Julius' life an absolute nightmare. He could wage war on the young man; he could pull his lawyers out of Julius' murder trial; or he could have some of his many people to go to Miami and murder his mother. Julius thought that he had gotten his mother out of the city and that she was safe, but there was very little that the Barrera's didn't know.

It wasn't that major though, and Mr. Barrera wasn't going to pursue any vengeance for Sleepy's murder. The things the young man had gotten himself involved in had caught up to him and cost him his life. His only real dilemma now would be whether to tell his sister the truth, or lie to her to make her feel better. He had always done what was best for the survival of his family, but if he told his sister that her only son had it coming, she would not only hate him forever, but she would mentally cave in. He couldn't take that chance.

He did, however, have working to his advantage the fact that she had no clue as to why and by whom he had been murdered. He would simply tell his sister that it was taken care of, and if she was true to form as she always was, she wouldn't want any details. She hated her family's business, but she tolerated it because it kept her satisfied in the lifestyle that she had become accustomed to.

"Flaco, get Julius and his brother on the phone and let them know that I wish to have a meeting with them," Barrera said.

"And if they refuse?"

"If they refuse, which I doubt they will, kill them and everything that they love."

"How can you be so certain that they won't resist, Mike?"

"Because, brother, they are the sons of Julius Gage Sr., and they are bred for confrontation. If they are anything like their father, they would rather stare death in the face than hide as if they were afraid. We'll give them the ultimate choice. We'll either continue to make money together, or they will die for the things they did to our *sobrino*," Mike Barrera said confidently.

The young men were dangerous and he knew it. He wasn't afraid of them; he was actually intrigued by them. Revenge kept them going and their hustle was fantastic.

Julius had made Devon his head of security so to speak, and Devon ruled with an iron fist. If they kept running their business as intelligently as they were at this moment, they would own Dallas.

Mr. Barrera liked the fact that the brothers weren't flashy and that they were smart about their finances. He silently hoped that the men would accept his invitation because he didn't want to have them killed, and he didn't want to lose the money associated with doing business with them.

Flaco picked up the phone and dialed Julius' number.

"Hello," Julius answered.

"Hello, Julius. This is Flaco. Mr. Barrera requests your presence at the compound."

"When does he want us to come?" Julius asked.

"He would like for you to come as soon as possible, *amigo*."

Flaco was silently fuming as he hung up the phone. If he had his way, he would do away with the young *miate'*. He was getting away with too much. Flaco didn't like the fact that his brother let the notion of Julius bringing in a lot of money keep him from avenging their nephews' death. He would have preferred for Sleepy's demise to come at their hands than to let him die by the hands of outsiders. He would bide his time until they slipped up, and when that happened he would be there to catch them and make them pay for crossing his family.

Chapter 8

Revenge Served Cold

Julius and Devon sat outside of Yellow Shoes' house. They had followed Detectives Sweeney and McVey there. Greed had a way of bringing out the rats in people. It had been months since Booty Green's murder, but the case was still looming over Julius' head. He needed to get something on these corrupt policemen to use as ammunition.

They sat for what seemed like hours outside of the pimp's home in a black panel van. It had been Angelica's idea to use Detective Sweeney's greed as his downfall.

Julius had called Sweeney from a pay phone across the street from the police station and told him that he had proof that he'd been set up by him. He also told him that he was going to Internal Affairs about his behavior. And as an added threat, he told him he had witnesses that were willing to come forward and testify on his behalf.

"What do you want?" Detective Sweeney had asked.

Julius knew that men like that respected one thing and one thing only; money. "Listen, Sweeney. I'm not above paying you for your time. I know Yellow Shoes is paying you, so whatever he's paying you I'll pay you double to make this shit go away," Julius told him.

Sweeney had taken the bait hook line and sinker. Julius knew that Sweeney being as greedy as he was, would run straight to Yellow Shoes to give him an opportunity to beat Julius' bid. And just as he'd suspected, Sweeney and McVey had left the police station soon after the phone call and drove straight to Yellow Shoes' home.

Julius had powerful, high quality microphones aimed at the house that were capable of picking up the slightest noise, so the entire conversation was easy to record.

They watched as Yellow Shoes greeted the detectives at the front door. Devon snapped a couple of pictures to add weight to their plan. It didn't take long before the men inside the house started incriminating themselves:

"What brings you gentlemen to my humble home?" Yellow Shoes asked.

Sweeney looked at the man with disgust. It irritated him when Yellow Shoes talked to him like he was better than he was. But he dealt with him because the man was very good at supplementing his income. "I got a call from your boy today. He basically said that whatever you're paying me he would double, so you have some decisions to make," Sweeney said incredulously.

"I have decisions to make? Are you trying to extort me, Sweeney?" Yellow Shoes asked. He had a smirk on his face that belied the seriousness of the situation.

The glance that Sweeney shot the pimp was cold and harsh. He hadn't come to the man's house to play games. He wanted money, and if Yellow Shoes wasn't willing to give it to him then he would take Julius up on his offer, and Yellow Shoes would be left on his own. "I'm not trying to extort you. I just want what I feel I have coming. You and I both know that Julius no more murdered his step-father than the man on the moon, and I wouldn't lose any sleep if your black ass spent the rest of your life in prison for murdering your so called friend," Sweeney spat.

"Don't come in my muhfuckin' house threatening me, cracker! If I go down, you go down! Remember that shit!" Yellow Shoes screamed.

McVey interrupted. "Listen, you two need to calm

down. The problem is not with each other, it's with that little gang banger, Julius. If he wants to give us money to make the case go away, then so be it. That shouldn't change our situation. Yellow Shoes, you keep giving us what our agreement is, and we'll just find another patsy to dump the murder charge on. It's as simple as one, two, three."

"Yeah, that's fine for y'all, but it still poses a problem for me. That little nigga will stop at nothing to get some get-back for his family's murder, so I'm still left wondering when I'ma hafta kill the little bastard," Yellow Shoes said.

Sweeney hated cowards. Yellow Shoes was terrified and it showed in his conversation. "We'll make sure he doesn't come after you. You just make sure you have that money ready every month like you always do. We'll take care of Julius and his brother. We'll make them think that everything is okay, and then boom! One day they'll have a gang related accident."

A round of hearty laughter filled the room.

Julius had everything that he needed in order to take care of the crooked cops. He cranked up the van and headed towards the Lew Sterrett Justice Center.

He and Devon entered the building and asked to speak with someone from Internal Affairs. Moments later a burly black man in an expensive suit came out into the lobby to greet the two men.

"How may I help you gentlemen?" the detective

asked.

"Is there somewhere that we can talk in private?" Devon said.

"Right this way, please."

They were led into an empty interrogation room.

"Okay, so what's this all about?" the detective asked.

Julius began by telling the detective how his stepfather had been murdered, and how he had been framed for the murder. But the look that the man was giving him told Julius that he didn't believe a word he was saying. He could only guess that people came in professing their innocence all of the time, so it wasn't surprising to him.

"Listen, I wouldn't be in here wasting your time if I didn't have proof," Julius said as he handed the detective a large manila envelope containing the recording and three pictures of the men together. "I'm not just trying to get out of something, sir. I'm actually innocent, and if you listen to this tape it will prove it."

"Okay, let me get a tape recorder. And young man, if what you're saying is true, you should feel like a real hero. Cops like this" he said pointing at the envelope, "give the rest of us a bad name."

The detective exited the interrogation room and came back with a tape recorder in hand. He took the tape from Julius, loaded it into the recorder and listened intently. If a picture was worth a thousand words, then seeing his expression had to be worth a million. "Do you have copies of this, son?" he asked.

"Yes sir, I do."

"I could go and arrest these men right now, but I want to get them with their hands in the cookie jar," the detective smirked.

"What do you have in mind, sir?" Devon asked.

"Well, I would like for you two to get in contact with the detectives and find out if they're ready to make a deal. If they say they are, offer them the pictures and recording, along with the money. If they go for it, we'll have enough to put them away for at least ten years."

When they finished up, Julius left the Justice Center feeling as though they had actually accomplished something. He would give Sweeney a call later on that night because right now he needed to meet with the Barrera's. He needed to clear this Sleepy shit up before it led to an all-out war.

They pulled into the Barrera compound unaware of what to expect. As they drove down the long driveway towards the house, it was obvious that both men were becoming more paranoid about the situation. But Devon pointed out to his younger brother, "Shit, if he was gonna kill us, he would've just sent his boys to do a nigga, you know?"

Julius had to agree, so the only thing left to do was play the waiting game and see what Mr. Barrera had in mind.

They rang the doorbell and were shown inside to

the dining room where Mike and his brother, Flaco waited for them.

"Hello guys. Would you like a drink?" Mr. Barrera asked.

"No thank you," Julius said. "If it's all the same to you, we'd rather get right down to business," he added.

"I think it is important to let you two know that from information that we have obtained, we are well aware that you were responsible, if not directly, for our nephew's murder," Mr. Barrera said.

"Actually, if you want to be technical about the situation, he was near death when we got to him," Devon said.

Julius went on to say, "We actually did him a favor by putting him out of his misery. And furthermore — "

Mr. Barrera cut him off before he was able to finish. "Julius, although I understand why Sleepy met his demise, I will not allow you to come into my home and desecrate the memory of my nephew!" the old man said excitedly.

"Mr. Barrera, with all due respect, your nephew was trying to have me killed because I do good business with you. I considered him a friend and he spit in my face. How would you have preferred for me to react?" Julius asked, bewildered.

Mr. Barrera studied the young man's face. Either he was really as fearless as he appeared to be, or extremely stupid. Mike Barrera had killed men for a lot less than murdering a family member, but the men he murdered hadn't made him millions of dollars. He wanted this to be over and done with, and get back to doing what he did best; making money. "That is neither here nor there, young Julius. What is important is moving past this mess that has been created and continue conducting business. I need your reassurance that this was only an isolated incident, and that you are willing to move on."

Flaco and Devon locked eyes. The skinny Mexican man made Devon uneasy, and there was something about the way Flaco had been eyeing his little brother that stirred anger in Devon.

"Is there a problem, *amigo?*" Flaco asked Devon.

"I was going to ask you the same question, man. I'm wondering why you're looking at my little brother like you have a muhfuckin' problem," Devon responded irritably.

"Now gentlemen, there is no reason to be rude to one another. My brother, unfortunately, is still reeling from the untimely death of a family member. He will in time get over it. But until that time comes, we must tolerate one another for the greater good," Mr. Barrera said and smiled.

"*Esto no es correcto. Estos hombres entran en la casa de nuestra familia, y vergüenza la memoria de mi sobrino y permita hacerlo en aras de un dólar!*" Flaco spat as he exited the room.

"What did he say?" Devon asked. He was getting

irritated with Flaco's disrespect, and it made his trigger finger itch.

"He will be just fine. He is just upset and feels that I have let you men get away with murder, so to speak. But no worries, Flaco is a loyal soldier. He is harmless unless I tell him otherwise. Nevertheless, our business here is concluded. Julius, Devon, there is no need to worry. Conduct your business as usual, and we should be just fine. Feel free to see yourselves out," Mr. Barrera, said dismissing himself from the room.

As they left the home, Devon looked at Julius and said, "Bro, you know that muhfucka Flaco is gonna be a problem, right?"

"Yeah, I know, but as it stands right now, big bro, we have a pass, so let's get this money before those shady bitches change their minds. We'll fuck with them until we get a stronger connect," Julius said.

The brothers jumped into the black van and drove off into the night, headed towards their women. It had been a long day of business, and it was time to relax.

******

Shayla wheeled the white Mercedes Benz to the corner of Gaston and Haskell Ave, and parked in the Good Luck Burger parking lot. She stepped out of the car and eyed the whores milling about inquisitively. Shayla was gorgeous and she knew it. Her ebony satin like skin glimmered against the moonlight. She'd chosen a soft yellow body suit that heightened her voluptuous body and accented it with an oversized turquoise belt with heels to match. The girls working the strip, watched Shayla post up on their stroll with a mixture of curiosity and envy. "Bitch you must not know where you at?" Candy said.

"Excuse me?"

"You heard her Ho this is Yellow Shoes' strip, whatever second grade pimp you're working for must have a death wish." Alicia said.

Shayla laughed heartily, "Bitch I don't need no pimp, I Ho for me and me alone."

Shayla smiled inwardly as the girls searched for words to combat what she'd just said.

"You rolling in a car like that just from selling pussy and you ain't got no pimp?" Candy asked curiously.

"Hell naw, what I look like giving some limp dick nigga my bread and I'm the one with that good good? Fuck that shit, it's my pussy, it's my money! If you Ho's wanna make some real money, let's spend a little time together."

Candy winked at Alicia, "Ok baby if you want to get into some freaky shit it's going to cost you $50."

Shayla nodded in agreement, "that's fine, get in the car and let's take a ride."

Candy and Alicia scurried towards the car like two eager children fighting over who would get a chance to sit in the front seat. Alicia made it to the front seat first and sank into the plush Italian leather seats.

"Oooh girl it smells good in here, what's that smell?" Candy said from the back seat.

"It's Vanillaroma," Shayla said.

Once the trio was inside the car Shayla drove away from the scene and they all laughed. The whole argument had been a ruse just in case Yellow Shoes happened to come to the stroll and noticed the two girls missing.

"So did you girl's get the nut? If you did I have $600 with your name on it." Shayla said.

"Yeah, Candy got it last night from that weak dick nigga."

Candy shuttered from the thought of the pimp touching her. When she'd first met Yellow Shoes, he'd wooed her, making her believe that she was the most beautiful girl in the world. He had taken her away from the country streets of Memphis and brought her to Dallas. The whole way there he had stopped along the way and made passionate love to her, essentially making her believe that she was his world. After they'd arrived in Dallas he'd changed. He'd introduced her to her *wife-in-laws* which were the other whores in his stable.

Yellow Shoes had changed almost instantly, but that had been eons ago. She'd seduced him the night before knowing that his routine would be the same. He'd had sex with her, humping ferociously as if he were an inexperienced teenager, bringing himself to climax practically as soon as he'd started. He'd given her the condom to discard, rolled over and started snoring.

"Yeah I got it girl," she said passing the sealed zip-lock bag to Shayla. It contained a sperm filled condom that had been tied in a knot.

"What are you going to do with it if you don't mind me asking?" Alicia said.

Shayla smiled at the girl but, didn't offer any information. The less people involved the better. She handed Alicia six crispy one hundred dollar bills. "However y'all decide to split it is up to you. When the shit hits the fan just act accordingly, and if you value the life that I am giving back to you, you will forget that you ever met me, do you understand?"

Chapter 9

All Falls Down

Yellow Shoes was fuming. How dare those peasant ass police try to muscle him! He paced back and forth across his immaculately clean white Berber carpet. His mind was twisted, and he couldn't think straight. It seemed to him like everyone was either betraying him or turning their backs on him. If they didn't recognize loyalty when they saw it, then fuck them!

In all actuality, he wasn't loyal and didn't give a damn about the idea of loyalty. It was a dog eat dog world, and if they knew like he knew, they would see that it was every man for himself. He would personally make everybody pay who had crossed him, and he would start with Julius and his brother. With them out of the way he wouldn't have any worries, and would no longer need the protection of Detective Sweeney.

But before Yellow Shoes went on his "Gage hunting expedition", he wanted to party; to go out with some of his bitches and really do it big.

Two of his girls entered the room. "Did you say something, Daddy?" Yummi asked.

"Did you hear your name, bitch?" he asked.

She abruptly turned away, mumbling as she left the room.

Any other time, Yellow Shoes would've followed the young Asian girl and slapped her across her mouth, but he wasn't in the mood.

The second girl, Alicia, stood idly by and watched the pimp intently. She didn't understand how he could be so cruel to them when they were the bread winners. He didn't show any love or concern for his girls, and that bothered her.

"What the fuck you staring at, ho? Spit it out!" Yellow Shoes shouted.

The young girl couldn't have been older than eighteen. She looked the pimp up and down as if to size him up. "Nothing!" she spat back disdainfully.

"Man, you ho's are gettin' beside yourselves. Go get the rest of them bitches so y'all can break bread," he said.

She turned to walk away, and was suddenly

knocked down by a slap on her cheek.

"Stand up, ho!" Yellow Shoes said as he towered over the young girl while leering menacingly. "Don't you ever in your muhfuckin' life look at me like that, bitch! You should be honored to be in the presence of a mack of my stature! Bitch, I was gettin' ho money when you were still blowing snot bubbles in your mammy's juice box! You ain't shit! You're probably one of the ugliest bitches in my stable, but the johns like that young, firm tight ass of yours, so your ugly ass is good for business. Now go do what I said before I kick you in your ass!"

Alicia looked up at the man through tear filled eyes. It had been a long time since a man had put his hands on her, and she had promised herself that it would never happen again. Here she was though, at the feet of a man that didn't give two shits about her. She held her cheek as she rose to her feet. She would do as she was told, but he would pay for hitting her for no reason. "Yes, Daddy," she said.

Moments later Alicia returned with the remaining seven girls in Yellow Shoes' stable. He sat back in his white, plush leather king's throne like chair with golden trim, and lit a Newport cigarette. One by one the women walked up to him and emptied the contents of their purses, as if to pay tribute to the man that was somehow responsible for their continued success.

Each woman's money was counted out in front of the pimp and the other whores. It was almost as if the man did it to show who was worth what within his organization. In pimp circles it was a well-known fact that whoever brought in the most money by turning the most tricks was considered to be a pimp's favorite bitch.

"Yummi, $1000; Alicia, $500; Candy, $100; Rory, $1200; Mesha, $1200; Ramona, $1000; Jasmine, $1500."

Yellow Shoes recounted the money over and over again. "Candy, are you holding out, ho? Everybody else made decent amounts of money, and you come bringing your busted ass in here with $100!" he said furiously.

"Daddy, it started raining and I—"

"Kill that shit, bitch. The other ho's went out the same time as you. You'll fuck around and find yourself turning two-dollar tricks out of your mammy's house like you were when I copped you!" he vehemently spat.

"No, Daddy, please!" Candy begged.

"Go get me a clothes hanger, bitch. The rest of you ho's are dismissed," he said.

The eight whores left the pimp to contemplate his next move. They didn't try to console Candy or rally around her. Instead they treated her as if she had some incurable disease that was somehow contractible by simply being too close to her.

Candy returned with the metal clothes hanger and began to undress. As she stood there naked, the cold air against her skin hardened her nipples and gave her goose bumps.

Yellow Shoes untwisted the clothes hanger until it

was as straight as an arrow, and whipped the young girl like a slave across her back and buttocks.

She yelped in pain as the hanger ripped into her young, soft tender skin. She just stood there; afraid to move for fear that any sudden movement would cause her master to become more enraged.

"Alicia, get your ass in here, bitch!" Yellow Shoes screamed. The depth of anger emanating from his voice caused Candy to flinch, and a small, barely audible squeal escaped her lips.

Alicia hurried into the room so as not to arouse his anger any further. "Yes, Daddy?" she asked in her sweetest and meekest voice.

"Take this bitch in the other room and put some salve on her bruises. I want this ho ready for work by nightfall. And since you two bitches are bottom earners, y'all can sell pussy to make up my money while the rest of us have a good time tonight."

Alicia hated Yellow Shoes, but she was afraid to leave. She'd heard stories from some of the other girls about what happened to ho's in the past who tried to leave him, and none of the stories had happy endings. Her only way out was death—either his or hers. And if the woman that had talked to them while they were turning tricks on Gaston Ave held true to her word then Yellow Shoes would be a distant memory. The woman had refused to give Candy and Alicia her name but asked if they wanted to make a quick $600? They'd both thought that it would be a quick tryst in the bed with another female, but the young girl had wanted information about Yellow Shoes, his friend Rabbit *and* a condom with Yellow Shoes semen in it. Well she was anxious and nervous, the woman needed to hurry!! She helped Candy gather her clothes and took her to the bedroom they both shared.

Yellow Shoes wasn't one for sentimentality, but he was proud of his stable. He had eight of the rawest bitches in Dallas. He didn't have any regrets or remorse about being hard on his girls, because the harder he was, the harder they hustled. "A ho with no instruction was headed for self-destruction," he had been told when he was first introduced to the pimp game. He had lived by that creed all of his life, and he saw no sense in changing it now.

Yellow Shoes stood in front of the full-length mirror, giving himself the once-over. He had to admit that there weren't too many cats in the pimp community that could touch his dress code. Most of the pimps in Dallas dressed like clowns to him. Their over-sized hats, loud jewelry and bright colors seemed buffoonish. He considered himself different. The loudest color he ever wore was a splash of yellow to signify his moniker. Other than that, he wore mostly earth tones and pastels.

Tonight he was dressed brilliantly in a white Italian cut linen suit, a white shirt and a yellow tie. To top off his outfit he added yellow, big block alligator shoes, and a white fedora with a yellow band. He knew that he was shining like new money.

He reached into his pocket and removed his wad of cash. There was $5000 in the knot. He wanted to show some measure of appreciation to his whores, and since they had been gracious enough to compromise their morals and dignity, he would reciprocate by spending a small amount of the cash that they'd earned for him on dinner and drinks.

After he was done primping in the mirror, he walked into the living room and took a seat on his throne. As was customary, the women all lined up single file to get the pimp's final approval of the attire that they had chosen for the night.

It was a spectacular ordeal. Each girl would meticulously go through her closet in hopes of picking out the perfect outfit. To wear something that he didn't approve of meant that they would be left at home to turn tricks until the wee hours of the morning.

Candy and Alicia were sitting on a nearby couch staring at the women as if wishing that they could somehow take their places.

"This ain't no Cinderella story. You two ho's go put on some working clothes," Yellow Shoes ordered.

The two girls moved hastily past the pimp and scurried to their bedroom like two frightened mice.

Yellow Shoes got up to examine the remaining females closely. He circled them like a vulture over his prey, and he couldn't find one female that wasn't dressed to his approval. "Alright, you ho's did good," he said. "Load up the two Lacs."

The girls all squealed in excitement as they made their way towards the garage that housed Yellow Shoes' extravagant fleet of cars. His Fleetwood Brougham's were his favorite. Whenever he and his band of bitches hit the town together, he would always take his Cadillac's. He knew that this was predictable, but predictable was safe.

He was chauffeured in his Caddy. It was yellow with a white top, and had white interior with yellow piping. The other car was the exact opposite. It was white with a yellow top, and had yellow interior with white piping.

Yellow Shoes always had the car that he was in lead his entourage of whores, because if by chance he saw something that he didn't like, his bitch, Rory who drove the Cadillac behind him, was trained to follow his lead.

Yellow Shoes planned to take the girls to Center Stage. It was a popular hangout among the pimps in Dallas, and whenever someone pulled up, it felt like Hollywood. A curbside red carpet, velvet ropes and bouncers greeted the arriving players. The average onlooker would stand to the right of the ropes, hoping for a chance to get in, while the pimps and hustlers would be ushered through the velvet ropes and immediately shown to their awaiting tables.

Yellow Shoes and his caravan of bitches made their way through the city streets. The bright lights from office windows bounced off of the asphalt to the tinted glass of nearby automobiles, and back to the asphalt again, creating an illuminated path along the rain-slicked streets.

As they neared the club, Yellow Shoes spotted his old friend, Rabbit. He had on his arm perhaps one of the most beautiful chocolate women that he had seen in a long time. Her features were soft but strong, and her body was perfect. She walked with a confident swagger, and the white stiletto heels that she wore only served to accentuate her ass that much more. She wore a firm fitting white mini-dress with a plunging neckline that seemed to make her luscious breasts protrude from her body. With every breath that she took, her breasts looked as if they were fighting to escape her constricting wardrobe. Her ass was like two perfectly molded mounds of pure glory, and with each bounce of her ass cheeks, Yellow Shoes felt his manhood twitch, not from horniness, but from the sheer excitement at the thought of the amount of money a trick would pay for a single sniff of the young tender. *This nigga's been holding out like a muhfucka!* He thought.

He sat at the red light watching Rabbit and the young girl enter the club.

To his left, from the corner of his eye Yellow Shoes

saw a white Mercedes Benz turning onto 2nd Avenue where Center Stage was located. The Benz parked in front of the club and a light, brown skinned man that looked vaguely familiar exited the vehicle and handed the valet his keys. A second later another man got out of the car.

Yellow Shoes' heart dropped to the pit of his stomach. It was Julius Gage. He looked so much like his father that it sent cold chills down the center of his back. *That's why that other nigga looks so familiar too. That must be his brother*, he thought. He instructed Yummi to turn left onto Hatcher. He wouldn't confront the men in a packed club. They drove down Hatcher headed for the freeway to go back to his home.

Yummi looked at her pimp in astonished bewilderment. He never missed an opportunity to be seen. "Is everything okay, Daddy? You look spooked," the girl said.

"I'm fine, bitch. Just drive," He mumbled. *Why are they at Center Stage? This can't be no fucking coincidence. Julius don't frequent this spot, maybe they were there because they knew I'd be there, maybe they are meeting with Rabbit and this nigga done sold me out!* Yellow Shoes was thinking.

Nevertheless, he wouldn't give them the opportunity to strike first. He would strike first, and strike hard.

As they made their way to his house and parked in

the garage, Yellow Shoes could see the disappointment spread across the face of each girl as they exited the cars.

"Yummi, I need you to get these ho's out on the track. There's money to be made," he said as he walked into the house.

Yellow Shoes went to his bedroom and closed the door. He sat down on the edge of his bed and stared into nothingness. *How can I get these little niggas before they get me?* He thought. "Think nigga! Think!" he said aloud.

He suddenly snapped his fingers and sprang to his feet. He hastily shed his clothes and replaced them with all black attire. He hated sneakers, but he put on a pair anyway. He rustled through his dresser drawers until he found a black ski mask and a pair of black gloves.

He then went into the garage and pulled the cover from a black Katana 1100 motorcycle. He turned the ignition switch and the bike roared to life.

He drove it out of the garage and stopped at the edge of the driveway. He got off of the bike and mounted the kickstand, reached into his pocket and took out a Newport cigarette. He leaned against the motorcycle while he lit it, and took a long, deep drag. Smoke from the cancer stick swirled lazily around his head like a smoky halo.

There were a lot of things going through his head, but the most important was fear. He hadn't known too much fear in his fifty plus years, so the feeling was relatively foreign to him, and he didn't like it.

He took one last deep drag from the cigarette, hot boxing it and causing the tip to glow bright orange before he flicked the butt across the fence into his neighbor's yard. His neighbor was an old, rickety, mean spirited woman named Ms. Krebs. She didn't like Yellow Shoes, and he hated her equally as much. "If she don't like my cigarette butts in her yard, fuck her! She can suck my dick!" he said. He got back on the bike, revved the engine and sped off into the night.

*****

Rabbit was feeling like a true player. It had been quite some time since a woman had come on to him, especially a young one as fine and sexy as the one he was with tonight. She was a true head turner, and as soon as they entered the club all eyes were on them.

They were shown to a table near the back of the club. The table sat atop a half stage and was positioned so that Rabbit and his date could see their entire surroundings. It was more like they were placed there so that everyone could see them.

Rabbit had never had as much attention as he was garnering at the club that night. He had always blended into the crowd.

The young girl with him cooed and giggled, and whispered in his ear. He was sure that she wasn't old enough to drink, but if she wanted a *sex on the beach*, then that's exactly what she would have.

A waitress carrying a drink tray chest high approached the couple at their table. "Can I get y'all a drink, sugar?" she asked.

"Um, yeah. Let me get a *sex on the beach* for the lady, and a VSOP and coke for me," Rabbit said.

The waitress nodded and disappeared into the crowd, delivering drinks to some of her other customers.

Rabbit's date was whispering things in his ear that he didn't think could come out of the mouth of someone so beautiful. "Oooo, Daddy, I want to feel you inside of me right now," she whispered as she let her hand glide over his stiff manhood.

Rabbit was anxious to leave the club, but first he wanted to have a few more drinks. He needed them to loosen up because he was intimidated by the young, sexy girl, and he wanted to be able to let go of all of his inhibitions. If necessary, he would pay for the privilege of lying with the tender goddess. He didn't want to question her motives, but in Dallas most of the women that came on to him were usually whores looking for a payday.

He hadn't met her in any of the usual locations that he occasionally met the working girls. He'd met this girl while he was at Valley View Mall trying to find an outfit to wear to the club. She had walked right up to him and volunteered to help him pick out clothes. She had even paid for it and said "a man as handsome as you should never have to worry about shopping for yourself."

She fawned over him like she had known him for years and he liked it. Hell, for that matter he was happy to have the attention of *any* female these days.

Rabbit had chronic low self-esteem. It wasn't that he was an ugly man, but living in the shadows of players like Yellow Shoes and Booty Green for so many years had dimmed his star, so to speak. So when she had phoned him later in the evening and invited herself along for the night he didn't mind at all, after all, she had been kind enough to pay for his outfit, the least he could do was let her see him in it, right?

The girl had exquisite taste in clothes. They looked as if they were a matching couple on purpose. He was wearing simple white linen slacks and a shirt, with no blazer. The pale green eel skin belt he wore matched the eel skin loafers that he wore on his feet.

The waitress made her way back to the table and served the drinks to the couple, as she turned to leave Rabbit gently grabbed the girls arm to stop her. "Wait, sweetheart. You forgot the money," he said, holding out a twenty dollar bill.

The waitress turned around. "Your drinks were covered by those two gentlemen," she told him while nodding her head and looking in the direction of Julius and Devon.

Rabbit followed her line of sight and spotted the two men. They sat at the bar looking at him and smiling as if they'd seen an old friend. Rabbit got the urge to rise and bolt from the club, but instead he decided to keep his cool and see how things played out.

"Maybe you should invite your friends over, Daddy. That was nice of them to buy us drinks," the girl with him said cheerfully.

"Naw, baby. Those are very busy men. Maybe another time," Rabbit responded. He raised his glass to the young men, who in turn raised their glasses, downed their drinks and walked out of the club.

Rabbit began to sweat instantly. *I hope those niggas ain't in an alley waiting for me when I leave this bitch*, he thought. He tried his hardest to keep the men off of his mind, but he couldn't.

"Can we dance, Daddy?" the girl asked.

He stepped out onto the dance floor with his date and moved in close to her, grinding and gyrating on her behind provocatively. They danced to three songs, and by the time they were finished, Rabbit was exhausted.

"Ooo, baby, if you fuck anything like you dance, I'm in for a real treat!" the girl said, licking her lips seductively as they moved through the crowd and headed back towards their table.

With every word that she spoke, Rabbit became more and more aroused.

She touched his hand as she looked into his eyes. "Don't you like me, Daddy?" she asked.

"Hell yeah, I like you! Shit, that's part of the problem!" he said.

"What you mean by problem?"

"I mean… I guess I'm just hoping that you like me for me, and you're not just tryna get some money out of me."

The girl folded her arms like a child and began to pout.

"What's wrong with you, baby?" Rabbit asked.

"You hurt my feelings, honey. I don't want your money, I want your big dick and I want your tongue, see?" she said as she grabbed his hand and guided it underneath the table and between her legs. "I don't have on any panties. See how wet you got my cookie?" she asked while looking deep into Rabbit's eyes. He thought she was wet because of him but in reality just the sight of Devon sitting across the bar in his black silk Gucci outfit had gotten her instantly aroused.

That did it! If they didn't leave at that instant he was going to explode. Rabbit removed his hand and licked his fingers. He noticed the excitement in the young woman's eyes as he licked her moisture from his fingers. *Oh, hell yeah! I'm finna eat this little bitch alive!* He thought. Rabbit was cunnilingus certified and he knew that once he put his tongue into any woman's juice box, they were hooked. It never failed. He was good at eating pussy and he knew it.

Rabbit took the girl by the hand, and she smiled as he led her through the crowd and out of the club. Once outside, he took a look around. He was buzzing, but he wasn't anywhere near drunk. He still had his wits about him, and he was on the lookout for Julius and his brother.

"Where are we gonna go, Daddy?" the girl asked.

"I got a little loft downtown. I'ma show you how a high roller does it, baby girl," Rabbit bragged.

The couple got into his black Lexus and drove towards downtown Dallas.

Shayla sat on the passenger's side of Rabbit's sports car and grinned at the man seductively. She knew how to take a man's mind away from any suspicions, and she was good at it. The business that she and Devon were involved in demanded that she knew exactly how to manipulate men and women alike.

She had watched Rabbit closely for a few days and noticed that he had the same routine day after day, and he was never with a woman. He had the look of depression and desperation, which told her that he was a very lonely old man. Spending time with him had confirmed all of her observations. He had been easy pickings. A little flirt here, a bat of the eyelash there, a simple brush of his sleeve, and he had fallen hard.

Rabbit pulled into the parking garage of the seven story brick loft on Elm Street in downtown Dallas. They rode the elevator up to the seventh floor, and the elevator doors opened up to Rabbits loft. He had the entire top floor to himself.

Shayla had to admit that the place was beautiful.

There was strategically placed frosted glass walls separating each room. He had elegant furniture throughout the loft, and most of the pieces looked very expensive. It kind of blew Shayla's mind because she didn't get an impression of exquisite taste from Rabbit. He struck her as an old, lascivious pervert that got his kicks from tricking off his money with young girls.

"Damn, Daddy! This is pretty. It makes me feel like you're too good for me," Shayla teased.

"Naw, sweetness. If you let me, I'm trying to share everything I got with you."

"Won't your friends look at me funny? I don't want people thinking I'm using you. You're paid, and I'm just a cashier at a grocery store," she said.

Rabbit took a hard look at the young lady. She was gorgeous. He couldn't imagine why nobody had snatched her up and made her their wife. He shook his head and said, "Don't be silly, pretty baby. Any one of those dirty old men would give their lives to be in my shoes right now. As long as you keep it all about me, I'll give you whatever you want. Besides I don't care what people think about me."

"I'm ready for you to use these," she said as she touched his lips with one hand, and his crotch with the other.

"Okay, baby. Let me shower and then we can get down to business," he said excitedly.

"Why don't we shower together?" Shayla asked.

Rabbit didn't waste any time getting undressed.

Shayla undressed and placed her clothes across a nearby chair. She could feel Rabbit's eyes on her.

Rabbit's mouth was salivating at the thought of tasting her, and at the thought of putting his semi-erect penis inside of her young, hot, wet twat. He watched as Shayla walked towards his bathroom. His heart was beating fast from the excitement and he tried hard to focus to no avail. He didn't want to cum too quickly when they started making love but he could feel his heartbeat in his shaft.

He watched her firm round ass as she stood in the bathroom mirror. When she bent over at the waist to start the shower, she exposed her full womanhood and he felt as though he would lose his load right then. She was shaved smooth, and the lower she bent the more of her luscious pink bubblegum colored slit exposed itself.

He walked into the bathroom as she stepped into the shower, and joined her. He kissed her neck and she shuttered. She reached down and stroked his hard dick with a soapy hand as she kissed him deeply.

After they finished washing each other, they exited the shower and headed to the bed, leaving a trail of wet soapy foot prints in their wake.

"Daddy, I want to get freaky with you. I want to show you exactly how much I like you," Shayla said in a husky voice.

"What you got in mind, baby girl because I got

some shit in that drawer over there."

Shayla walked to the drawer, opened it and gasped at the sight of the wide variety of sex toys the old man had in his possession. There were feathers, handcuffs, silk scarves, and vibrators of all shapes and sizes. *This nigga is a freak,* she thought as she giggled internally.

She grabbed a pair of handcuffs, two silk scarves and a ball gag. She walked over to the bed and playfully rubbed the silk scarf across Rabbit's genitals. She put the gag in his mouth and handcuffed him to his bedpost. Finally, she blindfolded him with one of the silk scarves. "Are you ready, Daddy?" she asked seductively.

"Hell yeah, I'm ready baby!" he responded.

She grabbed his penis and gently stroked it, and it stiffened in her hands. He wiggled from the pleasure of having her hands on him.

Shayla then walked over to her purse, removed a small .380 caliber pistol and a straight razor. She walked back over to the bed and let a single fingernail trace gently from Rabbit's balls up to his chest.

She reached up, grabbed the blindfold and violently ripped it away from his eyes. She pointed the pistol in his face and began to speak. "Let me tell you why you're going to die. You are a murderer and a thief. You are a liar and a cheat."

Rabbit shook his head from side to side as if to deny the accusations. His eyes told a story of complete horror and shock. He was terrified, and his body began to tremble.

"You murdered the Gage's because of envy, and whenever the day comes that my future husband and I decide to have children, they will never know their grandfather. And, for your part in depriving my unborn children of that pleasure, you have to die. Today your world crumbles and all falls down for you, Rabbit," Shayla continued. The voice of the sexy, timid girl that he'd met was gone; she spoke with venom dripping from her every word.

She put the gun on the floor and took his penis in her hand. With the straight razor she made one quick swipe and detached his manhood from his body.

Rabbit writhed in pain. He screamed in terror but his screams were muffled and barely audible. She removed the gag from his mouth, but he was in so much pain that he could no longer scream. He was in shock and lay still in a bloody puddle.

Shayla slapped him violently with the butt of the pistol, and his forehead gushed blood from the blow.

Rabbit began to cry and mutter under his breath. He was barely able to form a sentence. "Please, just kill me!" he whispered.

"Oh, I am, my love. No need to worry," the ruthless female said. Shayla walked to Rabbit's stereo system and turned up the volume, *it's a thin line between love and hate, it's a thin liiiiiine between and hate. The sweetest woman in the world can be the meeeeeanest woman in the world if you make her that way.* The *Persuaders* belted from beyond the airwaves. She walked back to him, put the pistol against Rabbits temple and pulled the trigger, and watched as his head jerked violently to the side, spraying blood and brain matter against the clinically white sheets.

Shayla smiled as she stared at him. She shoved his penis in his mouth. Blood still spewed from his wounds, and his body was twisted into a ghastly, contorted shape from the force of the gun shot. "I can see what's on your mind, freak," she said aloud.

She went to the drawer and removed one of his many dildos, along with a tube of K-Y Jelly. She flipped him over and violently rammed the dildo into Rabbit's exposed ass over and over again. She then took a turkey baster from her purse that was filled with semen and injected it into the dead man's rectum.

Shayla walked to the bathroom and showered, washing Rabbit's blood from her body. She put her clothes on and wiped the loft down for her fingerprints with the second scarf, making her presence unknown, careful to leave no traces of evidence.

She entered the elevator and left the crime scene totally unseen and undetected. Shayla walked to a payphone two blocks over and called the police. "911, what's your emergency?" the operator said from the other end of the phone. "Yes I heard two men arguing in my building and then I heard a gunshot, somebody might be hurt." She lied. "Ok we will get someone right out to you, what is the address?" the operator asked. "I am at 8670 Elm Street in the Quorum Lofts, but I'm not sure where the shot came from." With that said Shayla hung up the phone, walked another block and held a cab. She had committed murder on many occasions, but never in the name of love. She would die for Devon Gage, so killing for him was nothing. If necessary, she would put a bullet in the president himself if it meant keeping her man happy. Love had taken a hold of her, and there was no turning back.

Chapter 10

Watch for the Double Cross

Julius and Devon left Center Stage, elated. Devon was more excited than Julius because he knew how Shayla operated. She was a female version of him, and she would do whatever it took to complete a job.

"Man, I hope Shayla doesn't have any problems with Rabbit, bro," Julius said.

Devon looked at his brother and erupted into hysterical laughter.

"What's so funny, dude?" Julius asked.

"I'm laughing because you look all worried and shit. Ju, trust me when I tell you, Shayla knows how to handle her business, man. Believe it or not, she's more ruthless than me and you both put together," Devon said.

Julius trusted his brother, so if he had complete confidence in Shayla, he wouldn't question his judgment.

They pulled the white Mercedes into the plush suburban subdivision in North Dallas, not noticing the black motorcycle that had been following them since they left the club.

Yellow Shoes parked his Katana motorcycle and walked to the security gate. The only visible entrance was the gate for cars to pass through, but the wall surrounding the neighborhood was brick and only stood five or six feet high. He was older, but physically Yellow Shoes was still in excellent shape.

He walked back to his motorcycle, lifted the seat and removed his midnight black .45 caliber handgun. He checked the clip to make sure that it was full and put the pistol in the shoulder holster strapped to his torso.

He walked over to the brick wall and pulled himself up, paused at the top and jumped down to the other side. He stood up and brushed himself off while looking around to make sure his descent had gone unnoticed.

He walked up the dark winding road searching for the address that held his intended victims. The street was dimly lit, save for widely spaced residential street lights that cast an ominous glow along the path. He was careful to stay within the cover of darkness. It was important that he wasn't seen or heard, because he wanted the element of surprise. He rationalized that it would definitely give him the ultimate advantage.

Yellow Shoes stopped dead in his tracks. The brothers were standing by their car. They had yet to go inside of the house, and he wondered which would be more effective; killing them in their driveway, or inside of their home. He laughed silently and thought, *What difference would it make?*

He continued to creep under the veil of darkness until he was less than two hundred feet from Devon and Julius. The brothers talked for a few minutes more, and Devon disappeared into the house. Julius just sat on the hood of the car.

Angelica emerged minutes later, walked over to Julius and threw her arms around his neck. She stood between his legs, kissing her man.

Yellow Shoes looked on in stunned amazement. A small smile creased his lips as he imagined killing her, along with her man and his brother. *It's a shame to let that fine piece of ass go to waste, but if you got to go, you got to go,* he reasoned.

He seized the opportunity. He moved with cat-like swiftness towards Julius and Angelica. As he neared them he raised his pistol. From the distance that he was away from them, he could easily pick them off one by one, but he wanted Julius to watch him kill his girlfriend. He also wanted Julius to know who had taken the lives of everyone he loved. He would just have to go inside and kill Devon. The silencer on the tip of his pistol would insure that his presence went unnoticed.

The ambush startled Julius slightly. He jumped a little bit, but he wasn't afraid. "What the fuck are you doing out here, old man?" Julius asked with disgust and irritation dripping from every word.

"I came for your life, little bitch ass nigga!" Yellow Shoes snapped. "I'ma kill you, your little pretty ass bitch, and then I'ma kill your punk ass brother. I plan on eliminating your whole family and erasing your whole fucking bloodline. You muhfuckas are starting to bother me!" Yellow Shoes spat angrily.

Julius moved Angelica gently to the side and jumped down off of the car. "Now what makes you think you can kill all of us? The world ain't big enough to hide you. If anything happens to me or anyone else I love for that matter, my family will hunt you down," he said sarcastically.

"Little boy, you have no idea what I'm capable of. I'm still trying to decide whether I want to fuck that little bitch before I kill her or not," Yellow shoes said and laughed.

Julius was fuming. It was one thing to threaten him, but nobody threatened his Angelica.

Inside the house, Devon looked at the monitor. He was dazed and stunned with fear. He had never feared any man, but to see his only brother staring down the barrel of a gun paralyzed him with terror. Julius had been adamantly against installing the security cameras around the house, but now Devon was glad he had talked his little brother into it.

He took his chrome plated pistol from his waistband and headed for the back patio door. He made his way past the pool to the side gate leading to the side of the house. He gingerly lifted the latch to the gate as to not alert the old man of his presence. He crept through the gate and moved silently towards Yellow Shoes.

Looking past Yellow Shoes' shoulder, Julius noticed Devon coming around the corner of the house. He stepped in front of Angelica to block her line of sight. He didn't want her to see Devon, get spooked and give away his position.

"You can't protect that bitch, boy. After I've finished killing your black ass, I'll show her how a real man treats a ho as fine as her," Yellow Shoes threatened.

Devon raised his pistol and moved quietly behind Yellow Shoes. He put the muzzle of his 9mm to the back of the Yellow Shoes head and nudged slightly. "You ain't killing shit tonight, old man, unless you plan on dying too. Now, drop the muhfuckin' gun!" he said.

Yellow Shoes fought the urge to turn around. He knew without a doubt that tonight was his last night on earth. The boys would kill him for certain.

"Drop it, nigga! I ain't bullshittin'!" Devon said as he cocked his pistol to let him know that he was serious.

Yellow shoes bent down and put the gun on the ground.

"Now kick it to my brother!" Devon ordered.

He did as he was told, and Julius quickly scooped the gun up from the ground and aimed it at Yellow Shoes.

Devon moved to his brother's side to face the failed assassin.

"Jelly, baby, go inside and find the duct tape. I think it's in the kitchen drawer," Julius said.

Angelica stood there frozen with fear. She had never witnessed anything remotely close to this, and it had her both terrified and mesmerized.

"Angelica, go!" Devon said, snapping the young girl out of her trance.

Angelica disappeared into the house to do as Julius asked.

"What the fuck were you thinking, old ass nigga?" Julius asked scornfully.

"Fuck this dude, bro. Let me do him right now. He's on our property, so we're justified," Devon said mockingly.

Julius looked at Yellow Shoes closely. Fear was written on his face and he began to sweat profusely. His body was tense and he stood rigidly still, as if not to move would somehow give him the power of invisibility. "No, Devon, we ain't gonna kill this muhfucka. I got something better for this piece of shit," he said while smiling dangerously at Yellow Shoes.

"I don't want to die, youngster! Just let me make it and I promise this shit is over, man!" Yellow Shoes cried. "Y'all go your way and I'll go mine!" he whimpered.

Julius and Devon looked at one another and laughed. *Was this guy serious?* they both thought.

"Let us think about it. Hmm... no, that's not going to happen. You have to pay for your crimes and sins as we all must do, you stupid muhfucka!" Julius said insolently.

"Get in the house, dumb ass. You got balls coming here with this bullshit," Devon said.

The old man cried openly as he turned to go through the front door. "Man, please don't kill me! I'm sorry... I'm sorry! I'll leave and you'll never see me again!" he begged.

"Stop whining, dude. That shit is not cute at all," Devon said condescendingly.

They walked inside, and Angelica ran to Julius and hugged him tightly. She handed him the duct tape and stood back.

"Over there," Julius ordered Yellow Shoes.

Yellow Shoes walked towards the direction of the dining room and was instructed to take a seat. He did as he was told, and Devon began to duct tape him to the dining room chair. Devon tore off a piece of tape approximately six inches in length and asked him, "You have any last words, nigga?"

As he opened his mouth to speak, Devon slapped the piece of tape across Yellow Shoes' mouth, silencing his forthcoming words.

"Guess it wasn't important," Julius said, and he and his brother both laughed.

Julius walked over to the telephone on the kitchen counter and placed a call. "Detective Perkins, please," he said into the receiver.

Moments later, Detective Doug Perkins was on the other end of the phone. "This is Perkins. How may I help you?" he asked.

"Sir, this is Julius Gage."

"Oh, hello, young man. how are you?"

"I'm just fine; a little shaken, but I'm good. Listen, do you remember the third man, Yellow Shoes, whose voice was on the tape with those crooked cops?"

"Yes, I remember. Why do you ask?"

"Well he came to our house tonight and tried to kill us, but we overpowered him and he's tied up in our dining room."

"Hmm. It seems to me that they really want to keep you boys quiet. Do me a favor and keep him there until we arrive. I'm sure the homicide detectives would love to have a word with him," Perkins said.

"Yes sir. He'll be right here when you and the detectives get here," Julius said, and hung up the phone.

Yellow Shoes looked at the young man with a mixture of hatred and alarm. His biggest fear next to death was spending the rest of his life behind bars, and if they proved that he was responsible for the murder of Julius' family members, he would not only face prison, but he would be headed for death row.

"Why did you call the police, Ju? Don't you think we should just smoke this lame?" Devon scolded.

"No I don't, bro, because if we kill this fool, they'll investigate. And even though we're justified because he was on our property, they could still put two and two together and say we murdered this bastard in retaliation for our father's murder. At least this way we're clear and he spends the rest of his life in prison."

Devon nodded his head in agreement. His brother had a valid point. Why kill the man when life in prison was a virtual death sentence anyway?

Shayla put her key in the lock and entered the house. She saw Devon with his gun in his hand standing just outside of the dining room. "I'm home baby, what's going on?" she asked.

Devon motioned for her to join him in the doorway. "Hard day at the office, baby girl?" he asked.

"No, actually it was like cutting butter with a hot knife," Shayla said jokingly. She walked over to Yellow Shoes and knelt in front of him. "Well, hello, pretty boy! I didn't know I would be seeing you here. I just thought that you should know, your little boyfriend is dead!" Yellow Shoes' eyes bucked from the revelation. "Don't look so surprised. You heard me right. Your little booty buddy, Rabbit didn't make it."

Yellow Shoes was stunned. This was the beauty from the club, and she had killed his only friend.

"You know you should really be nicer to the girls in your stable. Alicia and Candy told me to tell you hello," Shayla said with a devilish smirk.

Yellow Shoes struggled against his bondage. He mumbled and cursed against the tape covering his mouth.

"You treated them like shit, so it was almost too easy to get them to flip your punk ass." Shayla felt a slight bit of arousal from watching the man squirm uncomfortably in his seat. "They were more than willing to give me a condom full of your semen and all the info that I needed for $600. I inserted that semen into his asshole after I murdered him. I must admit, it looks like a crime of passion."

Shayla continued. "All of your girls will testify that you saw Rabbit and I enter the club, and you abruptly made them all go home. They will truthfully state that once y'all got there, you changed clothes and left suddenly. You have no alibi, booboo, and your DNA is in and on the victim," she said triumphantly.

Yellow Shoes dropped his head. He knew that there was no way out of the situation. Even if he told the police what he'd just learned, there was no way that they would believe him.

"Oh, and one last thing. Candy called the police

and told them that you left home in a jealous rage because you saw Rabbit and I together, and she's afraid of what you might do to Rabbit. And they received an anonymous tip that two men were arguing in the building and that they heard gunshots. They're probably finding his bloody corpse as we speak," she said and giggled.

Julius looked at Shayla in awe. *How could she be so beautiful and dangerously ruthless at the same time?* He wondered.

"I told you, bro; no worries," Devon said.

There was a knock at the door, breaking up the awkward celebration. Angelica went to answer it while Shayla made her way upstairs with Devon's gun. It would also give her an opportunity to change clothes just in case they had a description of the outfit she wore when she was at the club.

Detective Perkins of Internal Affairs and two homicide detectives stood at the door and introduced themselves as they simultaneously showed Angelica their credentials.

Once satisfied, Angelica showed the officers into the house and led them to the dining room.

Julius was sitting on the granite countertop with .45 caliber pistol pointed at Yellow Shoes. Detective Perkins identified himself and Julius handed him the gun.

"You want me to cut him loose?" Devon asked.

"Sure, why not?" one of the homicide detectives

said.

"Julius, we need to talk," Perkins said.

"Okay, follow me."

The stocky detective followed Julius to an office downstairs.

"Are you paranoid about something, son?" Perkins asked motioning towards the surveillance monitors.

"No, but they came in handy as you can see," Julius answered, nodding in the direction of the dining room.

"Look, I don't know your story and I don't want to know it. The only thing I care about is putting two crooked cops away for as long as I can. If they want to live like criminals, they can live *amongst* the criminals. No cakewalks and no protective custody. But I need your help to do it."

Julius looked the detective over with a piercing mixture of trust and admiration. Under any other circumstances he would never help the police, but in this particular instance it was a justifiable means to an end. "Whatever you need, I'm with you. Just let me know what's up," he said.

"When we take Yellow Shoes downtown for booking, you can ride with me. We'll go to the station and place a call to Sweeney and set up a meeting. I'll give you a manila envelope full of marked money, and when he accepts it we pop his ass and it's a done deal," the detective said.

"I'm with you, Detective Perkins," Julius said as

they exited the office.

One of the detectives began reading Yellow Shoes his Miranda rights. "Yellow Shoes, you have the right to remain silent…"
Yellow Shoes stood up and put his hands behind his back. He was handcuffed and led to an awaiting unmarked police car. He had no words. He knew from experience that the police had a solid case. Even if the part about Rabbit wasn't true, they would never believe him because of the other charges he was facing. He sat in the back seat of the police car knowing that his life was over.

******

Julius joined Detective Perkins in his car. It was a huge difference being in the front seat. With no automatic locks and no handcuffs he felt like a snitch, and there was no way around the feeling. In South Dallas if you cooperated with the police in any form, you were considered a rat. But this was a different situation. He wanted to make Yellow Shoes pay for the things that he had done, but death would be too easy for the man.

Prison time for the pimp would be excruciatingly painful. Pimps and drug dealers were a different breed than most criminals. The money often came fast and plentiful, and the most painful thing about being locked away wasn't the loss of freedom, but more so the thought of all of the money that they were missing while incarcerated.

They pulled into the Lew Sterrett Justice Center

garage, and Julius was instantly nervous. There were two things that he hated; jailhouses and hospitals. His breathing increased almost to the point of a panic attack.

"Are you okay, son?" Perkins asked him.

"Yeah, I'm straight. I just don't like jails, you know?"

"That's a good thing. That means I never have to worry about seeing your face behind these walls."

"You got that right!"

Detective Perkins slapped Julius on the shoulder and said, "Good... good. Let's get this over with so that you can get home to your family. Your little girlfriend is a cutie. You're a very lucky young man."

"Yes sir, I know. Thank you."

They walked into the police station, and Detective Perkins stopped at a row of lockers and put his gun inside.

He pushed a button and a young white female correction officer sprang to her feet behind a thick pane of glass. She pushed a button on her side of the glass and a loud buzzer sounded, giving the men admittance into the inner sanctum of the jail.

The two men took the elevator to the 2nd floor in silence.

Julius' mind was working overtime. He was watching for the double cross. He kept imagining getting up to the detective's office and being arrested after he had voluntarily travelled to the station with him.

They reached Perkins' office and were greeted by an elderly white internal affairs detective. "Is this our informant, Perk?" the man asked.

"Hold up, sir! I'm nobody's informant!" Julius said firmly.

"I'm sorry, son. I didn't mean to insult you. I guess I'm so used to dealing with snitches and crooked cops that I forget my manners."

"It's cool."

"Alright then, let's get started. Can I get you anything? A soda, a snack?" Perkins asked.

"No, I'm good. I'm just ready to get this over with."

The detectives showed Julius to a conference room that resembled an interrogation room, except that this room was well lit. There were three telephones on a round wooden table in the small, concrete room. Each man took a seat, and Julius pulled a small piece of paper from his pocket. The paper held Detective Sweeney's direct number.

"Okay, Julius, all you have to do is call him and tell him you're ready to do business. Tell him you have $5000 ready for him, and that you're ready to meet," Detective Perkins said.

Julius picked up the phone and dialed the number. He was surprisingly calm as he waited for Sweeney to answer.

Sweeney answered the phone. His voice was groggy and he was infuriated, probably from the disrespect of being awakened at such an early hour. "Hello!" he screamed.

"Aye, Sweeney. This is Julius."

"Do you know what fucking time it is?" Sweeney asked crossly.

"Man, kill that shit. I got five stacks with your name on it, and I got more where that came from if you can take care of Yellow Shoes for me," Julius said, playing his role to a tee.

"Take care of Yellow Shoes, how?" Sweeney asked.

"I don't give a damn how, man. He's starting to get on my nerves. I'm sure you have your ways."

"You're fucking right I have my ways! A bullet and a bucket full of concrete, and that coon is history!" the old bigot laughed heartily; his voice coming to life at the prospect of a possible lynching.

"I need to drop this bread on you. So what's up?" Julius said.

"Give me an hour and meet me at the IHOP on Greenville Avenue. And if you want me to take care of Yellow Shoes for good, it's going to cost you $20,000," Sweeney said greedily.

"Alright man. I got the five right now, and we can talk about the other fifteen when I see you," Julius said, and replaced the receiver back on the hook. He looked at the detectives who had been listening and recording the entire conversation. They were both thoroughly impressed with the young man.

"You did great, Julius. He'll never know what hit him," Detective Perkins said.

Chapter 11

Crooked Officer... Crooked Officer

Sweeney pulled into the rundown two story apartments that his young partner stayed in. It looked more like a seedy motel than an apartment complex. He parked and walked the short distance from the parking lot to McVey's apartment. Sweeney looked around the complex in disgust. His face was contorted in displeasure from the foul odor of cat piss and overrun trash dumpsters. The putrid odor made his stomach turn.

He climbed the stairs, passing a grizzled drunk that had the rancid stench of MD 20/20 and shitty pampers. He reached apartment number 202 and knocked hard on the door, but there was no answer. Normally he would've called before coming to the young detective's home, but he was in a hurry and didn't have time for formalities.

Sweeney knocked again, this time more forcefully, and he heard a muffled rumbling on the other side of the door.

McVey answered the door in dingy boxer shorts and a sweat-soaked T-shirt.

Sweeney pushed past the young man and entered his apartment uninvited. The space was small and cramped, but neatly furnished. It was in total contrast to the disheveled and unkempt man who answered the door, not to mention the outside of the building. "Get dressed. We need to take a ride," Sweeney said.

"Where are we going at six o' clock in the damned morning, Sweeney?" McVey asked in a low hushed tone. He stretched, scratched his butt and smacked his lips trying to wake himself up.

"Julius has our money, and we need to get it before the little fucker changes his mind. I'll explain the rest on the way, so hurry up. We're running behind."

Sweeney made his way to the unmarked patrol cruiser and waited for McVey. He had no problem killing Yellow Shoes, or Julius for that matter, if it came down to it.

It took McVey fifteen minutes to emerge from his apartment in a totally different state than before. He had obviously showered and shaved. He also put on a dark suit and necktie. "So, what's the story?" he asked as he entered the car.

"Julius called me and said that he has five grand for us to come and pick up. He also said that he wanted us to take care of Yellow Shoes. I told him that it would cost him twenty grand."

"And you're sure he's on the up and up? I mean, how do you know that we can trust that little snake?" McVey asked. His concern was well placed, and the thought of meeting the young gangster on his terms made him nervous.

Sweeney wasn't worried about the fears of his partner. He was concerned about the money that Julius had for them.

They pulled into the IHOP parking lot and scanned the area feverishly as they parked the car. They spotted Julius standing just outside the front door of the restaurant's entrance. McVey hopped out of the car and beckoned for him to come over.

Julius walked over to the car, careful not to look guilty. If they suspected that he was setting them up, he knew that they wouldn't hesitate to murder him. "What's up, Sweeney? What's up, McVey? Ain't no sense in bullshittin'. I got five stacks, and like I told you on the phone, I'm sick of that muhfucka Yellow Shoes thinking he can get away with whatever he wants and operate with impunity."

McVey leaned against the car, folded his arms and

studied Julius. "So what exactly do you want us to do to the asshole?"

"I don't care what you do to his ass, honestly, as long as I don't have to deal with him anymore. We all know that he killed my fucking family and wasn't shit done. I'm not letting him get away with that shit," Julius said.

"I know, I know. You want your nigger vengeance, yada-yada-yada. I understand. You're right, he did kill your family and I protected him for a small fee. I don't like any of you people, so my services go to the highest bidder," Sweeney said.

Julius was dumbfounded. He couldn't believe how easy it had been to make the man incriminate himself. He handed Sweeney the envelope containing the marked money and asked, "How long before y'all handle your business with Yellow Shoes?" The question was rhetorical because he didn't need an answer. It was simply meant to disarm the detectives.

Sweeney opened the envelope and quickly counted the marked money "Don't you worry your pretty little head, black boy. That'll be one less nigger on the streets," Sweeney responded. "Just make sure you let him know that it was Julius that outbid his ass before you kill him." Julius said as he walked toward the restaurant.

*****

Detective Perkins and one of his coworkers were

sitting in a black surveillance van parked behind the restaurant, recording the conversation between Julius and the detectives. Perkins had strategically placed other IAD officers throughout the parking lot just in case things got out of hand.

Julius reached the back of the restaurant and knocked on the van door. "How was that?" he asked, climbing into the van.

"You did good, Julius. You did real good," Perkins said. "Okay, men, on my ready!" he said into his walkie-talkie.

One of the detectives in the surveillance team jumped the gun. He pulled his car up behind Sweeney's and jumped out with his gun drawn. "Get your crooked asses out of the car!" the young IAD officer screamed.

Perkins was beside himself with anger. He had explicitly said *on his ready*, which meant to wait for his signal. "That young bastard jumped the gun! All units move in! I repeat; all units move in!" he shouted into his radio.

Cars diverged on the corrupt detectives from every direction. Sweeney and McVey looked at one another in astonishment. "What the fuck is this?" McVey shouted. He was beyond nervous, his hands began to sweat and his underarms itched.

"What do you think it is? That little black son of a bitch set us up!" Sweeney said nervously.

"What should we do, Sweeney? I don't want to go

to prison." The young detective was on the verge of tears.

"I'm not going to prison, son. They'll have to kill me first. I'd rather be carried by six than judged by twelve," Sweeney said.

McVey looked at his partner who had a crazed look in his eyes. He had a look that spoke of low pay and too many sleepless nights. "I'm not trying to die for a few lousy ass dollars, Sweeney," he said.

"Do as you please, but I'm not going out like one of those low life drug dealing niggers!" Sweeney said as he reached between the seats of the car and grabbed his service revolver.

McVey looked at him with sheer terror and thought, *How could the man risk his life when they were clearly outnumbered?*

"Passenger, drop your weapon out of the window and step out of the vehicle hands above your head!" Perkins said into a bullhorn.

Onlookers had started to gather inside and outside of the restaurant, eager to see some action.

McVey did as he was told. He dropped his gun out of the window, opened the car door and exited with his hands held high.

"Driver, drop your gun out of the window and step out with your hands up!" Perkins said.

There was no movement inside of the car, so Perkins repeated his command, this time a little more forcefully. "Driver, drop your weapon out of the window and exit the vehicle slowly with your hands up!"

Sweeney took his service revolver and threw it out of the window. But unknown to the detectives waiting for him, he tucked his 9mm Ruger into his waistband and stepped out of the car. There was no way he was going to prison. As soon as the prisoners found out that he was an ex-cop they would kill him anyway, so he might as well go out fighting.

Once Sweeney was out of the car Perkins started barking orders again. "Passenger, interlock your fingers and walk backwards towards my voice!"

McVey locked his fingers and began walking backwards towards Perkins. McVey was livid, this couldn't be happening. He had become a cop to serve his community and make a difference, but he had allowed Sweeney to suck him into something that was clearly not his fight. He was trying to be a good cop and a good partner. Now it would cost him not only his career, but his freedom.

McVey was rushed and slammed to the concrete violently. The IAD detectives didn't have any mercy on the crooked cop as they handcuffed him and tossed him into the back of the squad car like a rag doll.

Sweeney was incensed. He had been set up by an eighteen year old gang banging drug dealer. He wished that he could take Julius with him when he died. *How dare that little bastard cost him his career!* In his twisted mind none of this was his fault. His greed and treachery had cost him everything.

After he stepped out of his car, he looked around and locked eyes with Julius. The teenager was in the van with Perkins. Sweeney hated the IAD. Their sole job was to ruin the careers of decent police. He spat on the concrete, and for a split second he wondered if he could get a clean shot at Julius, but decided against it. He would take his chances trying to escape, and if it didn't work he would die trying.

"Driver, interlock your fingers and walk backwards towards my voice!" Perkins said.

Sweeney interlocked his fingers, but he didn't move. Instead he stood there silently, waiting for an opportunity… any opportunity.

He dropped his hands and bolted for the wood line leading to White Rock Lake. He ran at full speed while bullets flew past him striking the trees and ripping through leaves as he sprinted frantically towards the woods. He had no idea what he would do once he reached the woods, but at least he could rest until he could gather his thoughts.

Perkins jumped out of the van, surprised by the old detective's audacity. He took aim with his AR15 assault rifle, looked through the scope and realized that it was now or never.

"*Crack!*"

The first shot rang out, echoing against the dense

woods. He'd struck Sweeney in the right shoulder as the detective zigzagged towards the wood line. Sweeney stumbled but he didn't fall.

"Shit!" Perkins mumbled. He sent out a second shot, this time taking aim at Sweeney's leg. He wouldn't give him the pleasure of dying. He wanted to send the officer away to prison for a very long time.

The round hit Sweeney in his left thigh, sending him tumbling to the ground. As he lay in the dirt, the two shots sent searing waves of agony throughout his body. He groaned in pain as he fought to sit upright. He reached for the pistol in his waistband but it wasn't there. He searched desperately for the gun. He scrambled to his knees and tried to focus. He could hear running footsteps drawing closer, and then he spotted it. The 9mm was just out of reach at the base of a tree.

Sweeney crawled sluggishly to his gun and positioned himself with his back against a tree. His breathing was erratic and he slobbered at the mouth like a wild dog. He could feel the earth moving beneath his body as the footsteps drew nearer. He struggled to focus and wiped the tears of pain from his eyes with his forearm. *Well, this is it,* he thought. He could feel the footsteps thundering towards him. He raised his left arm and aimed at the blurry, shadowy figures running towards him.

Sweeney felt the excruciating pain of a third gunshot before he heard the deafening crackle of the rifle. He was totally exhausted and could no longer fight. He closed his eyes to rest and drifted off into slumber, content with the notion of letting death take him.

Chapter 12

The Shit I hate

Julius and his family sat on the balcony of the Beacon Hotel overlooking the sky blue waters of South Beach, Miami.

Angelica and Shayla sat poolside playfully splashing their feet in the water.

For Devon it was a dream come true. Sun and sand, a beautiful woman, a growing family, and enough money to do whatever he wanted to do. He looked at his little brother and studied his face as Julius leaned over the balcony in deep concentration. "What's on your mind, pimpin'?" he asked, going over to his younger brother's side.

"Nothing much, bro. I'm just trippin' because our babies will be born a couple of months apart."

"Shit, who are you tellin'? This shit is blowing my mind. I can't believe I'm about to become a daddy!" Devon exclaimed.

"Yeah, real talk. So what's the plan for us now, big bro?"

"I was gonna ask you the same question. We both got bread and we're both having kids, so maybe it's time for us to chill," Devon said.

"Hey, don't forget that you both got down ass gorgeous females in your corners!" Shayla said, stepping up behind Devon wrapping her ebony arms around his waist.

"How could I forget, baby girl?" Devon said.

The sun was setting in the distance and the day couldn't be more perfect. Angelica and Shayla would both be starting classes at the University of Miami in the fall.

Naje' wasn't happy about Julius taking time off before enrolling in school, but he had to come up with a plan for making his money grow. Between college and growing his money, there was no debating which one took precedence.

He and Devon had a lot to discuss concerning money. Julius had no intentions of going broke anytime soon. He and his brother were inseparable, and every decision that he made lately concerned his brother.

When they sat down and contemplated relocating, it had been an easy decision. With both of their women being pregnant, their safety had become priority number one. They would do whatever was necessary to insure the safety of the girls.

Angelica disappeared into the penthouse suite to make virgin daiquiris for her and Shayla, and the telephone rang loudly, startling the young girl. She answered it. "Hello."

"Hello, may I speak with Julius, please?" the caller said in broken English.

"May I ask whose calling?"

"Just tell him it's an old friend." The accent was decidedly Spanish, but thick and choppy. The man's voice frightened her a little because there was no emotion in it, and his demeanor was cold. She walked to the balcony door, wondering if she should even tell Julius about the phone call. She knew her man was about his business, and if it was business and she didn't tell him, he would be beyond upset with her. "Julius, baby!" she called.

"Yeah, baby, what's up?"

"You have a phone call, sweets."

Julius walked over to his woman and kissed her on the cheek. He then pulled her closer to him and kissed her more passionately before asking, "Who is it, baby girl?"

"He wouldn't say. He would only say that he's an

old friend," Angelica responded nervously.

"All of my fucking friends are in this penthouse," Julius said. He picked up the receiver and listened. There was only heavy breathing on the other end. "Hello," Julius said, but not a word was spoken. "Hello!" he said again.

"Hello, Julius. It seems as though we have some business to attend to. If not for some of your loyal soldiers, I would not have known of your relocation to Florida," Flaco Barrera said.

"First of all, how did you get this number; and second of all, I don't answer to you! My business is with Mike!" Julius said angrily.

"Mike, as you call him, is—how should I say—indisposed at the moment."

"Well, when he's not indisposed have him call me. As long as you guys' money is right I don't know why we're talking. Until Mike is available, lose my muhfuckin' number."

Evil laughter bellowed through the phone. "It seems as though we are dealing with a lack of communication. Your dealings are with me now, young Julius, and you must pay in full for the death of my nephew. So, either we continue making money together or..."

And then there was silence. Only a faint click and then a dial tone.

"This bitch ass—" Julius screamed.

"Yo, who was that, bro? Devon asked.

Angelica and Shayla came in after hearing the commotion.

"Is everything okay, baby?" Angelica asked curiously.

Julius was just about to answer her when a knock at the door silenced everyone in the room. Both Julius and Devon grabbed their pistols and made their way to the door. The brothers gave each other a knowing look, and as Julius opened the door Devon snatched the man violently into the condo.

The mailman had to be at least sixty years old and was visibly shaken. He held out a large manila envelope addressed to Angelica Gray. There was no return address; only a smiley face where the address should have been.

Devon released the man and smoothed his clothing. "My apologies, sir. We thought that you were someone else," he explained.

"Yeah, well in the United States it's customary to ask who it is, and then open the door!" the rattled old mailman said angrily as he exited the condo.

Julius held the envelope in his hands and stared at it for what seemed like forever. Besides Mrs. Gray, no one else knew where they were... or so he thought. That was before Flaco had called his phone, and now Julius wasn't sure who knew what. If the package was from Angelica's mother there would be a return address on it instead of a smiley face.

Angelica stood nearby watching Julius intently. "What is it, Julius? Why do you look so nervous, boo?" she asked.

He handed her the envelope and watched her face as she read the enclosed letter. Her face was ashen as she dropped the letter and reached into the package to reveal numerous vividly colored photos. She stumbled back trying to find a place to sit down and grabbed her stomach. She was obviously agitated, and Julius was immediately worried.

"Jelly, what is it, baby?"

Angelica handed Julius the pictures. In them was her mother in various positions, being raped and tortured. Mrs. Gray was chained to a bed in what appeared to be the warehouse that belonged to the Barrera's. She was badly bruised and beaten.

The men in the pictures surrounded her and were taking pictures as if they were on vacation. They were smiling and holding the thumbs up sign.

It made Julius's heart drop. He flipped through the pictures, and the next one showed a man deeply penetrating Mrs. Gray. He had his manhood buried completely inside of her while two Mexican men held her legs open. Flaco was standing in the background with an ominous smirk on his face.

Mrs. Gray's eye's had been beaten shut, probably to keep her from identifying her attackers.

Julius could no longer bear to see his future mother-in-law being treated so badly. He dropped the pictures, picked up the letter and read it:

My dearest Angelica:

Chinge tu madre, puta! *Simply put, we are fucking your mother, and will continue to fuck and torture her until you convince your coward of a man to come back and conclude our business affairs. Your mother is a tasty treat, and I have no problems spraying my seed deep into her love hole; that is, of course, until she begins to bore me, at which time my only choice will be to kill her.*

So, if you want your mother to see that poquito bastardo negro *that you carry in your womb, tell Julius he needs to get to Dallas, and soon.*

Sincerely,
Flaco

Julius let the letter fall from his hand. His blood was boiling. It had never occurred to him that Mrs. Gray was in any danger, and now he felt like it was his fault. He knelt down in front of Angelica and gently grabbed her arm. "I'm sorry this is happening, princess. This shit is fucked up," he said softly.

Angelica pulled away and looked at him. She knew

her man, and she could see the hurt and anger in his eyes. But her hurt, anger and worry were too great to be concerned with his feelings. She needed to lash out, and in a small way she felt as though Julius's lifestyle had done this to her mom. "Julius, I don't care what you have to do or how far you have to go, but you need to fix this!" she screamed.

She began to sob uncontrollably. "Fix it, baby! I can't handle this shit! I'm pregnant, and this is supposed to be the happiest time of my life, and here I am worrying about whether my mother will be alive to see her grandchild come into this world!" she cried. "I have always, since we were kids, trusted you; put my complete faith in you, and now is no different. Please, baby. Please bring my mother home. Besides y'all, she's all I got."

Her words rocked Julius' core. They cut deep, mostly because he knew what she said was true. She had always been in his corner and had never let him down. He had caused this by not tying up loose ends, and now he would be responsible for undoing what Flaco had done.

"I'm going to lie down. I feel lightheaded," Angelica said.

"I'll walk you to the bedroom, baby. And don't worry, we'll fix it. I promise," Julius said, and took Angelica's hand as he led her to their bedroom.

Once out of earshot, Shayla spoke. "Gage, we need

to go to Dallas and snipe those fuckers one by one. This is bullshit."

"I agree, baby, but knowing my little brother the way I've come to know him, this is a situation where he's going to want to get his hands dirty," Devon said.

"Yeah, but they don't know me, so we have an advantage. Plus, don't you think they're gonna be waiting for him?"

"More than likely yeah, they will but, we have something that they don't."

"What's that?"

"The element of surprise, baby. The element of surprise."

Shayla nodded her head in agreement.

Julius walked out of the bedroom moments later and motioned for the couple to meet him on the balcony. "She cried herself to sleep, bro. We gotta get some get-back. Those bitch ass Mexicans need to know that they can't just treat a nigga any kinda way!" he said. His anger was evident.

Devon hadn't seen this side of his little brother, and he liked it. He didn't believe that he was soft, but he didn't look at him as too hard either. Julius had told him stories about his capers, but to Devon they were just that... stories. This was the "Gage fire" that he wanted to see, and seeing it made Devon proud. "It is what it is, baby bro. If you want us to, me and Shayla will go take care of the Mexicans and get Mrs. Gray back," Devon offered.

"Nah, dawg. I've known Mrs. Gray since I was in the third grade, so ain't no way in hell I'ma miss my opportunity to set shit straight. I want Flaco's bitch ass to know it's me."

"So, how are we supposed to pull this shit off? I mean, it's not like we're dealing with any nickel and dime hustlers, bro. You already know that the minute we step off of that plane they're gonna know we're in town," Devon said as he fired up his blunt.

"That's the beautiful thing, playboy. We won't fly into Dallas; we'll fly into New Orleans and drive the rest of the way. That way we can move the way that we need to; strictly under their radar."

"For you to be the little brother, you're a smart little nigga, man," Devon said to him, and then turned to Shayla. "You heard him, baby girl. This is where your expertise comes in handy."

"I'm already on it, Gage. I'll be on the first thing smoking to the *Boot* in the morning." She disappeared inside the condo so that she could make the necessary arrangements.

"Listen, Julius. I don't know how much Pops told you about the family, but if the Mexicans are as dangerous as I think they are, we're going to need some help."

Julius knew that his brother was right. He was hot headed, but he was nobody's fool. If they went into this situation half-cocked, it could be a fatal mistake.

Duddy and D-Train were dangerous in their own right, but Flaco and his people were heavy hitters. They were worlds away from drive-by's and corner hustling. If Julius and Devon were going to pull this off, they would need professional help. "Dev, what you got in mind, bro? I don't know much about the family. The only one on Daddy's side of the family that I knew was Uncle Charles, and he died with Daddy," he said somberly.

"I guess me being in the D, I was exposed to more of the family. Man, we have two uncles in Detroit that are raw in the paint... I mean on some black mafia shit. They have sons around our age too, and all those niggas are gangsters. All it'll take is a phone call, and I guarantee they're coming."

"That's what's up! Man, we have to let my mama know what's going on so she's on point. If anything happens to my mom, bro..." Julius' voice trailed off as if lost in the fading daylight of the approaching Miami night.

Devon patted his little brother on the back. There was no need for Julius to finish his sentence, because he already understood.

"What I don't understand is if these muhfuckas are such big gangsters, then why in the fuck haven't they tried to avenge Uncle Charles and Daddy deaths, bro? I mean, I don't know these niggas from Adam, so help me understand," Julius said, clearly irritated.

"That I can't answer. But I didn't know who killed them until you told me, so maybe they still don't know. Either way it goes, we need to make that phone call and get shit popping."

"How many of them are there?" Julius asked curiously.

"Well, there's Uncle Eugene and Uncle Otha Lee, and between the two of them they have six boys," Devon said, and put fire to the tip of the blunt and inhaled deeply. He blew the smoke out through his nose and hit it hard again before he continued. "There's Demetrious, Tommy Lee, Marty, Junior, Keith, and Ray. Those niggas are about their business, bro, so I'm sure as soon as we explain the situation they'll be on the first thing smoking."

Devon offered Julius the blunt. Julius wasn't a big smoker, but the way that he was feeling made him want to smoke just to relax. He took the brown stick and inhaled deeply. The grayish-white smoke swirled around his head.

"Hold up, lil' nigga! That's big boy shit right there. Don't be hitting it too hard, rookie!" Devon laughed.

The laughter sent Julius into a hysterical fit of giggles. He hadn't laughed in quite some time, but it was more refreshing to have someone to laugh *with*. "I got this, dawg!" he said as he hit the blunt again.

Julius' laughter was quickly replaced with an overwhelming sense of gloom as he looked out over the balcony onto Ocean Boulevard. "Man, this shit is too much, Devon. I mean, don't get me wrong, I'm all in, but this shit is taking a toll on me. I just graduated from high school, my nigga, and me and Jelly are supposed to be on our way to Atlanta to enroll in school. But instead, I'm here with my brother that I barely know, planning a murder. I feel like an old nigga." He shook his head in disbelief. "Is this what life has to offer, Devon? Is this what my life is supposed to be, bro?"

Devon moved next to Julius on the balcony. "Listen, fam. After this shit is over we'll look back on this like one bad dream. But in the meantime, we have to handle our business. Those Mexicans won't rest until you and all those that you love are dead. Since we know that, we have to strike first. If you cut the head off, then the body will follow. I love me some me, so I ain't gonna let anybody hurt me. And since you're now a part of me, I won't let anyone hurt you either. But if we don't go to war now with those people, we are dead men walking and you know it!" he exclaimed.

He took another drag from the blunt and blew it in Julius's face to get his attention, and playfully punched his brother in the chest. "I don't know about you, but I got a baby on the way, and I got a whole lot of living to do, pimp!"

Chapter 13

What Kinda Bird Don't Fly?

Yellow Shoes sat in the small, two-man cell reading a letter from his lawyer. The overwhelming stench of hot piss, mildew and fecal matter combined with the aroma of Irish Spring bath soap made his stomach turn. *This is bullshit,* he thought to himself. He had allowed his anger to derail his plans, and gave Julius the opportunity to set him up. *"You reap what you sow,"* is what he had been told as a young man coming up.

This was different though. Yellow Shoes had to admit that he had underestimated the much younger man. He had gone into the situation hoping that his plan would work but Julius had come into the situation working his plan.

He looked around at his sparse surroundings. The gunmetal gray walls combined with the dimly lit lights made the cell seem smaller and gloomier than it actually was. He sighed heavily.

Yellow Shoes had hoped for good news from his lawyers, but the letter only served to make him angrier. The initial letter was standard lawyer speak, but the end of the letter is what infuriated him:

> *...In all actuality, this situation doesn't look favorable for you. As your attorney, I would urge you to allow me to come to a plea agreement with the District Attorney.*

> *David C. Goldstein, Esquire*

Yellow Shoes stood up and glared at his celly lying lazily in his bunk, reading the *Dallas Times Herald*. He despised the man although he barely knew him. What he did know was that his name spoke for itself. *What kind of grown man calls himself "Dirtbag"? "Douchebag" was more like it.* Yellow Shoes snickered at his own wit.

"What's so funny, celly?" Dirtbag asked.

"None of your fucking business, nigga. Don't worry about what the fuck is happening down here."

The venom in Yellow Shoes' voice wasn't missed by the recovering dope fiend. That was the primary reason for Yellow Shoes' contempt for the man. He could tolerate whores, pimps, hustlers, gamblers and thieves, but he despised fiends. Any man that would allow a habit to make him suck another man's dick wasn't his type of people.

Dirtbag sucked his teeth and lay back in his bunk. He didn't understand why Yellow Shoes looked down on him. He hadn't always been a crack head. He had once been a drug kingpin with plenty of everything; money; women; clothes and some of the most exotic cars that money could buy, but he had fallen victim to the first rule of the dope game: "Never get high on your own supply". Who was Yellow Shoes to think less of him? Shit, he was just a pimp! He sat on his lazy ass and waited for women to sell their bodies and bring him their hard earned money.

Yellow Shoes was beyond angry. He tried to search his mind desperately to make sense of the things that had taken place. In his mind there was no way that it should have been so hard to eliminate a teenaged threat. But somehow the boy had gotten the upper hand, and Yellow Shoes cursed himself for slipping. If he was going to escape this situation, he would have to use every ounce of his brain. Getting mad would only serve to hinder his progress, and progression was the key.

Texas was notorious for their outlook on the death penalty, they would give you the needle for spitting on the sidewalk and with the current charge of capital murder he was sure to face a lethal injection.

But what irritated him most was the fact that his name was smeared throughout the streets of Dallas. He had never once in his life so much as looked at another man in *that* kind of way. But in the streets of Dallas though, the rumor mill was always right. The streets had condemned him as a gay pimp who had killed his gay lover. Everyone knew how close he and Rabbit had been, and now in their minds the closeness made sense.

"Chow time!" came the call from an elderly black CO's steely voice.

Yellow Shoes stared out into the dayroom and watched as an assortment of criminals made their way to the bars to receive their ration of soggy chicken fried steak, powdered mashed potatoes, and molding bread. As a treat they had also included what looked like butterscotch pudding. Yellow Shoes learned from his first trip to prison that you never ate the pudding. Convicts worldwide knew that pudding in prison was nothing more than lubricant for the sick and depraved. The kitchen workers would use the pudding to jack their dicks and skeet into the dessert to hide the evidence. At least that was the rumor. But whatever the case, Yellow Shoes wasn't taking any chances.

Yellow Shoes couldn't shake the feeling of dread as he moved through the dayroom. He had made his fair share of enemies in his lifetime, but none of them, big or small, gave him the feeling in his gut like Julius Gage. He was afraid of the young man, and it bothered him, not because fear was new to him, but because his fate rested in the hands of a child — a teenager that had gotten the upper hand.

Yellow Shoes got his tray and made his way through the throng of small cliques that filled the dayroom.

The Mexicans congregated amongst one another, speaking their native language.

The whites huddled in groups eyeing anyone of a different ethnic background curiously.

The blacks, as usual, stood around eyeball fucking everyone in the dayroom, maybe from the anger of their impending trials, or maybe as an ultimate show of testosterone.

There was something about being in jail that caused a man to reflect on his past actions, whether good or bad.

Yellow Shoes settled into a corner where he was able to see the entire dayroom. With his back against the wall, he buried his head into his tray and devoured his meager meal.

His mind wandered back to Chele. He had actually loved the woman once upon a time, as she had loved him. But Julius Gage, Sr. had entered the picture with his cocksure swagger and stole her love. Of course Julius hadn't wanted her, but that hadn't stopped Chele from pledging her undying love for the man. Yellow Shoes hated Julius for taking Chele's love from him, and he was all too glad to help get rid of the problem.

In a society where self-worth was determined by the pigment of your skin, Julius should have been on the bottom rung, the only place in Yellow Shoes' eyes for a smut black nigga from the country.

His childhood and his upbringing was one of the many reasons that he held such contempt for his rural raised counterpart. He'd been raised on a farm like many southern black men. His family had been share croppers for generations and he was the son of a devout southern Baptist preacher. When Yellow Shoes was sixteen years old his cousin had come to their small dwelling in Crockett Texas and pretty much turned him out. His cousin wasn't more than a teenager himself, but he was from the fast streets of Chicago and had introduced Yellow Shoes to the pimp game. "Listen lil' nigga, it's pimpin' with me you dig? Ho money is sho' money and I keeps me a knot. When you decide to get some real money ol' country ass nigga give me a call." His cousin had told him. That was more than forty years ago and Yellow Shoes hadn't stopped pimping since.

His mind shifted to Rabbit, his loyal player partner. Sadness overcame him. Julius Jr. and his band of misfits would have to pay for what they'd done to his best friend. Everything had started with just him and Booty Green, but Rabbit had come along and solidified his place as a true friend to them both.

But now Yellow Shoes was alone, had no friends,

had no whores, and had no money. Yellows Shoes reached into his commissary bag and pulled out a crumpled letter. It was from Candy and Alicia.

Dearest Yellow Shoes, by the time this letter reaches you I hope that you are getting everything that you deserve you rotten bastard.

We are writing you to basically say that we know what you did. You killed Rabbit out of jealousy because you saw him with that fine ass girl that night that we went out. Considering the fact that you're never coming home Alicia, myself and the rest of the girls have gone our separate ways.

Yummi and that other sucker ass chink broad kept your house. Me, Alicia and the rest of the girls sold the cars, your motorcycles and your jewelry and split the money. We have a new Daddy now! I'm sure you remember pretty ass Silky Slim? Well we gave him all the proceeds from your "yard sale" and he was more than happy to take in six fine, topnotch bread getters. It was his idea that we write you out of respect. If it had been up to me I would've left you wondering but, our new daddy is a real nigga, unlike you who wouldn't know how to pimp a real bitch if she came with instructions. I hope they give you the death penalty you rotten, murdering, homo motherfucker!!!

Always, Candy

PS. This is Alicia, Shoes, on behalf of the rest of the girls I would like to say fuck you and have a nice life and Silky Slim said to tell you, don't drop the soap bitch ass nigga, you wasn't no pimp you was a rest haven for ho's.

He was all alone, possibly facing the death penalty for a crime that he didn't commit. He couldn't even call one of his whores, because he had treated them so badly that they had all left the minute he'd gotten locked up. To make matters worse they had chosen the one pimp that they knew Yellow Shoes hated and was afraid of.

His thoughts were interrupted by background chatter and whispers; murderous whispers that spoke of impending danger. Without warning or provocation, a young burley albino kid stood menacingly over Yellow Shoes, glowering angrily at the man. "What's happening, youngster?" Yellow Shoes asked curiously.

"Not much, old school. You mind if I cop a seat with you?"

"No, not at all, playa. It's a free country," Yellow Shoes said, returning to his tray of mush.

Casper sat across from Yellow Shoes, making small talk and trying his best to feel him out. Fate had a way of dealing certain cards, and the cards were most certainly falling in his favor.

With the money that Casper made in juvenile, he had been able to hire a jailhouse lawyer when he was shipped to Beto I Prison Unit. His prison attorney had been more than willing to draft the paperwork necessary to have his case looked into, especially after Casper had dropped $500 onto his books. He had been tried as an adult, although he was a juvenile when the offense occurred. If his sentence held up, then he would spend the rest of his life in prison. If by some miracle the courts decided that he should have been tried as a juvenile, he would be a free man on his eighteenth birthday.

Julius had held true to his word when they were in juvenile together. After Julius left the confines of the Texas Youth Commission, he'd left Casper in charge of a lucrative contraband-filled empire. He'd even been able to convince Miss Caine to start a savings account in the free world for him. He simply paid her $10 for every $100 that she deposited for him. She was in his corner full throttle, knowing that he was approaching his eighteenth birthday.

Miss Caine knew that Casper was a virgin, with the exception of raping the corpses of his two dead sisters. But the possibility of plucking the much younger man's cherry was too big of a temptation to resist. The promise of Casper's albino dick had her willing to do any and everything that he asked, and more.

Going into juvenile, Casper had been a withdrawn, chubby preteen, but five years into his sentence he'd transformed his once pudgy body into a chiseled mass of flesh and muscle. At seventeen years old he had grown into quite an impressive and imposing figure.

As he stared at Yellow Shoes, he was overtaken by the urge to end it all. His loyalty, however, belonged to Julius and 357um, and Julius had given him explicit instructions to wait for his word concerning the matter. The big homie, Julius wanted the man to suffer horribly, and Casper knew plenty of ways to torture a man.

Prison was overrun with books, and one of his favorite books was *Torture and Slaughter*. He knew that he was sick for the way that he thought, but he couldn't help it. Casper had an insatiable appetite for death, and he needed to feed his hunger. Until Julius gave the word though, he would simply get as close to the old pimp as possible.

Yellow Shoes met the boy's gaze and was startled by the coldness in his soulless eyes. The young man couldn't have been more than eighteen years old, but he had the eyes of a seasoned killer. If the boy showed promise, Yellow Shoes decided that he would take him under his wing; he was almost desperate for a friend.

He then chided himself for being so lonely as to allow a youngster that he barely knew, make such an impression on him. But truth be told, his eyes said that he was a killer, and Yellow Shoes could use that kind of protection if he went to prison... *If* he went to prison was the key phrase.

Yellow Shoes had no intentions of dying in prison. He would have to formulate a hell of a plan to walk away from his situation, and he knew it. Julius Gage had to be dealt with harshly, and he would not give him the satisfaction of being able to say that he won.

Chapter 14

Najé Goes Ham

Julius pulled his new BMW 750i into the parking garage of Naje's high rise condominium complex and parked. With the amount of trouble brewing, he felt uneasy about his mother living there with no security. He sat quietly for a minute trying to gather his thoughts before Devon broke the eerie silence.

"Are you okay, my dude?"

"I'm straight; just worried about my mom. I mean, if it was that easy for them to get to Mrs. Gray, how hard would it be to get to my mom?" Julius asked.

"Yeah, I feel you. That's why I want to eliminate this problem quickly."

Julius knew that his brother was serious. He wished that his relationship was as strong with his other brothers and sisters as it had gotten with Devon. Out of his two brothers and three sisters on his mother's side of the family, he only had contact with two of them.

Kolby and Katrina were twins that couldn't have been more different if they tried. They were five years older than Julius, and only spoke to their younger brother under strained circumstances. They had been raised by their father, Amos Gandy.

Julius Sr. and Amos Gandy had never seen eye to eye, and that hatred spewed over to the siblings. In fact, the relationship between Najé, Julius Sr. and Amos Gandy had been the rift that had led to Julius and Najés divorce. Kolby and Katrina looked upon Julius as a symbol of menace, and in their opinion, their mother and father's marriage and Julius Jr.'s subsequent birth served as a reminder that their father had no place in their mother's heart.

As a preteen he had missed the twins terribly, but as he got older those feelings subsided as he came into the realization that his siblings looked at him as an outsider.

Kolby was a low ranking hard head for the Black Gangster Disciples, and had no ambition and no money.

Katrina—or Kat as everyone called her, was a dope-fiend. She had been a crack head since age sixteen. Julius loved Kat because she was always sweet to him whenever Kolby wasn't around. Kolby called the shots for the twins, so whenever he was around, Kat and Julius' conversations were sketchy; almost as if she was afraid to let Kolby know that she loved her younger brother. When she was alone she would call Julius, and they would literally talk on the phone for hours about nothing and everything. *Oh well, fuck 'em! I haven't needed their asses in eighteen years, and I don't need 'em now,* he thought.

Julius and Devon greeted the Spanish doorman, Oscar as they entered the building and headed towards the elevator. As they made their way through the lobby, the brothers looked at one another. They both had the same gut-wrenching feeling that they'd had at Julius' graduation. It was odd how they could communicate without saying a word, and instinctively, they split into two different directions; their eye's darting swiftly and carefully from resident to resident, searching their faces for any sign of discord. Satisfied that they were in no immediate danger, they met back at the elevators.

As the elevator signaled its arrival, they stepped to either side of the doors, waiting for them to open. When the doors slid open, Najé stumbled out into the lobby in a daze. She was covered in blood and was holding a butcher's knife. The color was drained from her face. She looked ashen, as if she had seen a ghost.

Julius grabbed her and pulled her to him. "What's wrong, Mama? Are you hurt?" he asked.

Devon stepped inside of the elevator and looked around. There was no sign of struggle inside the small, confined space. "Miss Najé, are you alright? What happened?" he asked.

There was no answer. Najé just walked dreamily to a leather couch nearby and sat down. She began to speak, but her words were barely audible. "I killed someone... or at least I think he's dead. His body is still in the condo, I ran baby! He wasn't moving Ju." She said between sobs.

Devon and Julius exchanged wary glances. They knew that whoever she had stabbed to death had been sent by Flaco. "Somebody call the police!!" Julius shouted, "Don't just stand there gawking and shit, call the fucking police!"

Najé looked exhausted and confused. Her hands trembled violently as she reached out to touch Julius' face. The sight of his mother covered in blood and holding the bloody knife sent chills through his body. Flaco had gone too far. He wasn't allowing Julius to bring the fight to him. He completely initiated the altercation.

Looking at his mother Julius felt a pang of guilt for getting her involved in this madness. More so, his blood was beginning to boil. Flaco had overstepped his bounds, and he would pay with his life. He would make certain that it was a slow, painful and agonizing death.

Miami was a culturally diverse melting pot. It

wasn't uncommon to see any nationality at any given time. In Texas, Julius had only been exposed to blacks, whites and Mexicans, but in Miami it was different. Haitians, Jamaicans, Puerto Ricans, Cubans, blacks, whites, Asians, etc. all congregated and coexisted in the sprawling metropolis. The only color that mattered in Miami was green. Julius couldn't distinguish between a Mexican and a Cuban, so in his eyesight anyone with Latin blood flowing through their veins was suspect.

Julius looked towards the large ornate brass and glass doors of the lobby of the high-rise and saw two detectives, accompanied by four uniformed officers. They were headed towards the trio. He was immediately alarmed because the two detectives looked Latino.

"Mrs. Green, I'm Detective Hidalgo, and this is my partner, Detective Garcia. We need to go to your apartment to have a word with you. Hopefully we'll have this matter cleared up and you can get on with your normal routine."

"Normal? Normal, sir? With all due respect, someone just tried to kill me! He may or may not be dead in my apartment, and you say that I should get on with my normal routine?" Najé stated flatly.

"Forgive me, ma'am. In no way was I trying to be insensitive to your situation. I only meant that we do not wish to keep you any longer than we need to, that's all," Hidalgo said.

The uniformed officers began to take statements

151

from the other tenants in the lobby. Since they weren't used to such a brazen crime in the luxury high rise complex, they eyed Najé warily as she made her way to the elevator with the two boys and the policemen.

The ride to the tenth floor of the Sand Dune Condominium Complex was silent, except for the hum of the elevator's motor.

The group reached apartment number 1065, and the policemen entered first with their weapons drawn. In the living room in front of a large window overlooking South Miami Beach lay the body of Flaco's hit man.

"Excuse me, Mrs. Green. I'm going to have to call this in," the detective said as he pulled out his radio. "We're going to need a forensics team and a bus at 814 Ocean Boulevard," he said into his radio.

The dispatcher confirmed this, and the radio fell silent.

"Okay, Mrs. Green, if you don't mind, let's start at the beginning, shall we?"

Najé nodded her head. She knew that it was going to be a long day, but she had to get on with it. She was angry and frightened at the same time. Maybe if she told them what had happened, her emotions would take a back seat.

"I was sitting on my balcony drinking a mimosa, when I heard the doorbell. I went inside thinking that maybe it was Julius and Devon. I don't know why I didn't look through the peephole. I guess it was because I was expecting my boys. At any rate, I opened the door, and as soon as I did this man came rushing at me," Najé said, pointing to the man that lay motionless on her floor.

"Go on," Detective Garcia said as he scribbled quickly in his small notepad.

"Well, he scared the shit out of me, and I started to fight him back. I think it must've surprised him that I didn't just give up, because he kind of stepped back and looked at me like 'This bitch is crazy!' I broke away from him and ran into the kitchen and grabbed a knife. He was calling to me as if he was taunting me. 'Puta!' he'd say; or 'Cabrona, where are you?'" Naje explained as she wept softly.

"Ma'am, did it not occur to you to call the police instead of taking the law into your own hands?" Garcia asked.

Najé rolled her eyes at the man and sucked her teeth, "Mr., I don't know what planet you live on, but it kind of slipped my mind, seeing as this son-of-a-bitch was trying to murder me. Next time I will be sure to say, 'Hold on, Mr. Killer! I have to make a phone call!'"

"No need for sarcasm, ma'am. You said 'next time'. So, is this something that happens often with you people?" Garcia aked.

Devon spoke up. He didn't like police as it was, and he especially didn't care for this one. "Hold up, playboy. You're talking to her like she is a damn suspect or something. She's the victim; or did they not teach you how to spot the difference in the academy?" Irritation and contempt dripped from Devon's every word. He couldn't believe his ears. If this was the way that they did things in Miami, he knew that he and Julius and the girls had to find some other place to settle down.

"Mr. Green—" Garcia began.

"It's Mr. *Gage*," Devon said, correcting the portly detective.

"Well, Mr. Gage, we have to cover every angle and every avenue to accurately assess the situation. This is a murder investigation, so why don't you let us do our job?" Garcia was fuming. He didn't know why, but the young black man had gotten under his skin. Something wasn't quite right about the boy, but he wasn't there to pass judgment; he was there to investigate a murder.

"Investigate these nuts, officer!" Devon said coldly, and motioned for Julius to meet him on the balcony.

Everyone in the room chuckled quietly, except for Garcia. The statement wasn't funny, to him, and he resented his partner's laughter.

Devon and Julius stepped onto the balcony, and Devon lit a Newport. "Man, this is some bullshit! They're shooting at my mama like she did something," Julius said.

The detectives eyed the pair curiously, but until they knew more they would treat the two youngsters as concerned sons.

"Where were we, Mrs. Green?" Hidalgo asked.

"Anyway, I had the knife in my hand, and as soon as he turned the corner with the gun in his hand I swung at his arm. He dropped the gun and I ran towards the door, but he grabbed me by my hair and slammed me to the floor. He was coming at me..."

Najé choked back tears and continued. "He was coming at me as I was scooting backwards, and he lunged at me. I just closed my eyes and pushed the knife towards him. I could feel it going in, sinking into his flesh and scraping past his bones. He grabbed me around the neck and I pushed harder. He must've realized that I had stabbed him because he tried to roll off of me and I rolled with his ass and kept stabbing him until he stopped moving." She was crying more hysterically now as she recounted her story.

Devon and Julius re-entered the room in time to hear the end of her story.

The forensics team arrived and was shown into the living room to examine the corpse and gather evidence.

Najé was thoroughly exasperated by the whole ordeal. The quicker that it was over with, the better. She, Julius and Devon sat idly by while the policemen performed the arduous task of investigating the homicide.

The two Latino detectives shared hushed whispers with a member of the forensics team, and after what seemed like an eternity they turned to face Najé. Hidalgo stared at her for a long moment before saying, "Mrs.

Green, we may have more questions for you. Please take my card, and if there is any more information that you can think of to help in the investigation, please don't hesitate to call."

As if on cue, the fat detective, Garcia added, "Yes, and don't leave town. Stick around just in case we need to question you further." Naje' grimaced, she was agitated with the plump detective.

Julius made a motion towards the detective, but he was stopped short by a wave of his mother's hand. She knew that the policemen were beginning to irritate the brothers, and the last thing that she needed was for one of them to get into trouble. Although Devon wasn't her biological son, she felt a certain obligation to the young man because of her past relationship with his mother.

"Detective Garcia or whatever your name is, last time I checked my birth certificate said that I was a grown ass woman and although I have no plans to go anywhere if I choose to take a trip I am free to do as I damn well please." she said.

Hidalgo handed Najé a business card as they were leaving the spacious condo. After his partner had stepped out and was out of earshot, he turned to Najé and said, "I want to apologize for my partner's behavior. I'm not sure why he's being so callous, but, I can promise you that it will be dealt with, ma'am."

"His attitude doesn't bother me. I'm 'Queen Attitude'," Najé responded, and closed her door, ending the conversation.

Devon walked to the door and opened it. He looked down the long, elegantly carpeted hallway towards the elevators and locked eyes with Detective Garcia as the elevator doors slid closed. He needed to make sure that the police weren't camped outside of Najés place, trying to ear hustle. "Miss Najé, you should grab a few things and come over to the crib with me and Julius," he said.

"Yeah, Mama. I would feel a lot better if you were at the house with us and the girls. Besides, I really need to talk to you about some things," Julius added.

'That's fine, baby. Let me grab some of my things and I'll be ready, okay?"

Julius would have to let his mother in on the whole ordeal. It was neither safe nor fair to keep her in the blind after the fight had been brought to her doorstep. His mother knew that he wasn't an angel, but she didn't have the slightest clue who he really was. He would start at the beginning and lay it all on the line. After all, she was his mother, and she would love him regardless. But for his own peace of mind he needed to give her insight as to just how much he had grown to be like his father.

There was trouble brewing, and for the safety of everyone involved — especially his mother — he would have to come clean.

Chapter 15

Blood-4-Blood

As long as Flaco could remember, he had always held his brother, Mike in the highest regard. But now his thoughts of him were tarnished. He couldn't understand how Mike could look their sister in her eyes, see the pain of losing her son, and not want revenge. Mike was adamant that he didn't want Julius touched, and it had caused a rift in their otherwise peaceful relationship.

He was at a crossroads in his life, and it bothered him to no end. Their entire way of life could be in danger by letting Julius walk away.

The fact that Sleepy had been killed as some type of tribute to Julius didn't sit well with the young Mexican gang members in Dallas. Furthermore, if the Barrera brothers let him walk, their street credibility would cease to exist. There were faint mutterings in the streets of how they were letting the young *miaté* get away with murder. There was talk of how they sacrificed family for the sake of the almighty dollar. None of this was true, and it infuriated Flaco.

Their last argument had escalated after he had informed his older brother of the teacher, Mrs. Gray's kidnapping and periodic torturing. "I built this family business, and I will not allow you to tear it down!" Mike had shouted.

"If it had not been for me, you would still be changing tires for measly pesos, *panzon,* so keep your self-righteous indignation to your fucking self!" Flaco retorted.

The argument had erupted into punches being thrown, which was something that had never occurred between the brothers.

Mike would not concede to Flaco's terms, and Flaco's pride was hurt. He sat brooding and wondering how he could possibly make his brother see things from his point of view.

But Mike Barrera was as stubborn as they came, and he was very close to making his brother hate him. Mike had some nerve telling Flaco that he would not allow him to ruin the family, but it was quite the contrary. Mike would be the one to destroy what they had both worked so hard to build. Admittedly, Sleepy had crossed the line. His acts had been disloyal and treacherous, but family was family and blood was blood. Julius would pay for Sleepy's life with his own.

******

Mike Barrera was antsy as he sat in his study, pondering his next move. He had given Julius his word that he was free to leave the organization when he saw fit to pursue other things. Mike was fully aware that the events that Flaco had set into motion would cause major problems with Julius, because the young man was immensely loyal. The kidnapping of Mrs. Gray had in all probability angered him, not to mention caused confusion in his young mind.

Mike knew Flaco all too well. His brother would lure Julius back to Dallas under the guise of coming to the aid of his future mother-in-law. Once back in Dallas, he would kill Julius, and nothing Mike said could prevent it.

Flaco's relationship with the men in their organization far exceeded his. Mike's weight in the family had been diminished because the men looked at him as "the bank" — the money behind the cartel — and in their eyes, Flaco was *El Jefe'*. He was the one that they feared. His brutality was legendary, and they feared him wholeheartedly.

I'm older. Maybe I should retire to Mexico, Mike

thought to himself. But just as quickly he dismissed the notion. Why should he be the one to concede and relinquish the cartel? No! Flaco would have to bow down and listen. It was about appearances, true, but more so, they had to be smart in business. Albeit illegal, it was still business, and to hit Julius would create an all-out war with the Crips in South Dallas. They would lose hundreds of soldiers in the fight just to prove a point.

Most of their men were young and loyal, and would fight until their last breath. But most of them also had families and loved ones who depended on them for emotional and financial support.

He needed to make Flaco understand that they would lose more than they gained by his blind fury.

******

Flaco walked into the warehouse where Mrs. Gray was being held captive. His soldiers were sitting around. Some were watching television while the others were playing cards. In Spanish, he instructed his men to leave him and Mrs. Gray alone. They obeyed without hesitation. Their loyalty would be invaluable in dealing with Julius and his brother.

He turned his attention to Mrs. Gray. The teacher shifted uncomfortably under his gaze. Even underneath the dried blood and bruises he could see her exquisite beauty.

Mrs. Gray had been stripped naked, and her feet

and hands were bound with dirty ropes. She lay there unable to cover her nakedness. Her hands were tied to the railing of the cot above her head, and her legs were tied at the ankles to either side of the cot, exposing her bubblegum pink slit.

Flaco studied her body for a while, noticing that it was surprisingly taut for her age. Her body and facial features belied the fact that she had a daughter that was on her way to college.

"Well, well, well, Mrs. Gray. It seems as though we have quite the dilemma. You want to go home, and I want your future son-in-law dead. Julius has made some very important enemies. I hated to drag you into this, but this was my only means of bringing him out of hiding."

Mrs. Gray stared at the Mexican man. *How could such coldness and acrimony live in such an absolutely gorgeous man?* She sighed. "I don't know who you are and I don't care to know, but I can tell you this; if you let me go now, there is a chance that I may be able to convince Julius and Devon not to kill you."

Raucous laughter bounced from the walls of the warehouse. "My dear sweet lady, you cannot kill what is already dead. Julius killed me the day that my nephew died." Flaco moved to the side of the cot and sat next to her. He caressed her inner thigh and said, "You know, it is a shame that I am going to have to kill you. You are truly a thing of beauty."

He let his fingers slip inside of her love nest,

withdrew them, brought them to his lips and slipped one of them into his mouth.

Mrs. Gray watched the man in amazement. He was her captor and she had been raped and tortured on his command, but his touch stirred something inside of her. She was filled with loathing and contempt for him, but she was also very turned on. A small gasp—an almost inaudible moan of pleasure—escaped her lips as she squirmed uncomfortably. Her juices had begun to flow, and she cursed her libido. Her sexual appetite had been insatiable since turning forty, and she couldn't seem to get enough. "Do you like what you're tasting?" she asked

"Indeed."

"Then I suppose that it is a shame that you have to kill me, especially since you like what you've tasted, *and* you seem to have the ability to make me so wet," she said coyly. There was lust in her voice and desire in her eyes as she opened her legs to reveal her moisture. A small sticky bead of pre-cum glistened beneath the folds of her pussy lips.

"You *want* me to rape you, my love?" Flaco asked curiously.

"You can't rape the willing, baby. But then again, I've always heard that Mexicans had two fatal flaws that as a woman, I find it hard to deal with. Number one; I heard that you all have extremely short dicks, and number two; I've heard that you guys can't eat pussy," she teased.

Flaco was amused by her brashness. "Is that so? You have such a filthy mouth for such a beautiful lady. And they allow you to teach our children with that dirty mouth of yours?" he laughed.

As if on cue, he stood up and dropped his perfectly tailored slacks to reveal a fully erect penis.

Mrs. Gray gasped from the sight of it. It was nothing like she had heard or imagined. His engorged member was at least eight and a half inches long, and the sheer thickness of it was mesmerizing.

Flaco unbuttoned his silk shirt to reveal his toned body, complete with a bulging six pack. He stood before her in all of his glory, stark naked. The veins ripped through his caramel shaft, calling to her and pulsating ever so slightly and beckoning for her to take him into her moisture. "Mrs. Gray, I am guessing that we can put your first myth to bed," he teased.

She was in awe. His manhood was gorgeous, and under different circumstances she would have loved to have his dick for her own personal enjoyment. But as it stood right now, she simply needed to fill her greed. She also had to use every ounce of her being to survive so that she wouldn't die in an abandoned warehouse.

Chapter 16

Confessions

Julius stood in his kitchen with his brother, mixing an E&J and coke for his mother. Devon was truly living up to his words. He'd told Julius that until the situation was put to rest, he was going to be his shadow. He hadn't let Julius or Najé out of his sight since earlier that morning, and Julius welcomed the concern.

At this particular time his mind was on how he could explain to his mother the events that led up to the present. He didn't know how she would see him after he was finished explaining, but he didn't want to keep secrets from her any longer.

Shayla and Angelica were sitting on either side of

Najé, trying their best to comfort her when Julius walked into the living room and handed Najé her drink. He was a grown man now, and the responsibility was his to make sure that his family was safe. Having Devon made things less complicated, but ultimately the responsibility was his and his alone.

The lessons that his father had taught him came rushing back at him like a tidal wave: "Be intelligent when you check a man. Men can respect intelligence even when ignorance is expected," his father had said. From his deathbed he told Julius to never be ashamed of the things that he chose to do. Rather, strive to be the best in those things. He was a damn good hustler, and his bank account reflected it.

Julius took a deep breath and prepared to bare his soul to his mother. His confession would either bring them closer together or tear them apart.

He took a seat in the overstuffed leather chair directly across from his mother. He stared at the plush, cream colored Berber carpet, ashamed to meet her gaze. He was her youngest son, but what he had done and seen was more than enough for a person his age.

Devon beckoned for Shayla and Angelica to follow him to the balcony.

Najé watched Julius intently. She knew her baby boy, and something was stirring in his young mind. She could almost see the wheels turning in his head. He had grown into a handsome young man, but his facial features told a story just like they did when he was a child. His dark, cocoa colored eyes were hidden behind a furrowed brow, and were burning holes into the carpet as he kept his gaze trained on the floor. "What's wrong with Mama's chocolate chip?" she asked.

Julius nervously wrung his hands as he spoke. "Ma, I'm nobody's angel and I've done some pretty foul shit—excuse my language—but I've always tried to be a good person. I tried to grow into the type of man that a mother could be proud of."

"I am proud—" Najé began, but Julius cut her off.

"Just listen, Mama. Please. The things I've done in the past are directly responsible for the things that are happening in the present. What happened at your condo wasn't some random coincidence. It was a warning shot sent to me. There are very powerful people that want me dead, and they're using you and Mrs. Gray to make their intentions clear."

"Mrs. Gray?" Najé asked.

Without uttering a word, Julius picked up the manila envelope from the coffee table and handed it to her. She looked at Julius and then at the envelope, and then back at Julius again. She felt a rush of adrenaline, as if she should be doing something; doing anything but having this conversation with her son... her baby boy.

She opened the envelope and gasped in horror. Mrs. Gray was being sexually tortured by a gang of men. A lump formed in her throat and she was unable to swallow.

"Mama, me and Devon are going to Dallas to fix this. Mrs. Gray is all that Jelly has, just as you're all I have."

Najé understood instantly. Julius was not only his father's namesake, but he carried the same unbridled loyalty that had been Julius Sr.'s greatest strength *and* his greatest weakness.

There was nothing that Najé could say that would sway his decision. Life was about choices, and his mind was made up.

He walked to the kitchen and poured himself an E&J on ice. He then took a seat next to his mother and started at the beginning. He began by telling her about his many sleepless nights as a kid, wishing that she was there. He spoke of how he would cry himself to sleep most nights from missing her. He explained how his sadness had turned to anger because he felt like she loved his siblings more than she loved him.

Najé sat attentively as her son recounted his troublesome youth. She watched him break down and cry like a newborn baby when telling her how he, Shy and some other friends had gone on a robbing spree, kicking in the doors of the Jamaican dope spots that had ultimately gotten Shy killed. He'd felt directly responsible for the young boy losing his life.

He explained to her how he had come to meet Sleepy and his introduction to the Mexican Cartel, and how Sleepy had met an untimely demise.

He told his mother that not only was Angelica pregnant, but Shayla was pregnant as well. He explained how his life belonged to his unborn child.

Everything had been laid bare, and all of his cards were on the table.

His words spoke volumes to Najé. She realized after their conversation that he was more mature than she'd thought. He was a fifty year old man trapped in an eighteen year old's body. He was a tortured soul, and a young man cursed by his own intelligence, but blessed and protected by God.

By the time he finished talking, they were both in tears.

"Baby, I want you to know that I can't and won't judge you. You're not a baby anymore, and as a man I know that there are things that you must do. If I had my way, I would ask that you handle this situation differently, but you do what you feel is best. You're my last pea from the pod, baby boy, and I love you with everything in me. I would die to protect you, Julius. Just know that. I love you, Chip."

"I love you too, Mama."

"And Julius?"

"Yeah, Ma?"

"When you get to Dallas, be careful, baby and don't leave your enemies behind. Always protect what's yours Choc, don't give them the opportunity to harm your family."

Julius nodded his head. He understood that in his mother's own way she was giving him her blessing.

As they both stood and embraced, he towered over her 5'3" frame. He was most certainly not a baby anymore, but he would always be her baby... her "Chocolate Chip".

******

Julius stared at Angelica through the sliding glass door leading to the patio. The pregnancy had given her a radiant glow, and watching her reminded him of ballerina. Her every move seemed to be planned and flowed effortlessly, from the way she moved when she walked to the motion of her hand as she carefully brushed the silky ringlets of her hair from her face. She was poetry in motion, and she was carrying his child—his first born—his namesake, and he would shower his child with the same love and affection that his father had shown him. Whether it was a boy or a girl was of little importance to Julius. As long as his baby was healthy he would be happy.

He slid the door open and stood motionless, watching his wife to be.

Angelica noticed him eyeing her and smiled. "What are you staring at, Mr. Gage?" she asked.

"I'm staring at you, Mrs. Gage!" he shot back.

Angelica stood up, wrapped her arms around him and kissed him passionately. "I'm sorry I snapped at you, babe. I'm just really worried about my mom."

"I already know, baby girl. No need for apologies." Truth of the matter was that Julius was never one for arguing. Besides, Angelica was right. He needed to fix this situation.

"Bro, where's your mom?" Devon asked.

"She might have gone to lie down. I think she's feeling that 'Easy Jesus'."

"Easy Jesus?" Shayla asked, obviously lost on the slang.

"Yeah, baby. 'Easy Jesus' is what street niggas call E&J!" Devon laughed.

They all erupted into hysterical laughter at Shayla's lack of knowledge.

Then Julius launched right back into business mode. "How do you want to handle this, Devon? I mean, I'm thinking we can leave the girls here with Mama and scoot to Dallas and take care of business."

"Yeah, we can hit New Orleans by plane and drive the rest of the way to D-Town, take that muhfucka out of the game and be back before the weekend," Devon said. His adrenaline was pumping in overdrive. Killing was exciting for him. It was the best high he'd ever had.

Angelica watched the brothers and was growing increasingly more agitated. "Um, excuse me. I'm loving the way that you Gage men are talking about Shayla and I as if we weren't here," she said.

Shayla saw her chance and chimed in. "Yeah, on

the real, what makes y'all think we want to be sitting up in this apartment waiting for someone to come and chop us up?" she quipped.

Devon raised his hand as if he were a third grade student. Everyone turned to look at him, "Uh, Shayla baby, this is a condo. Broke niggas stay in apartments," he said jokingly.

"I'm serious, Gage! They already sent mail to our place and tried to do Miss Najé in her 'condo', so they obviously know how to get at us," Shayla said.

Devon knew that Shayla was right. It had been too easy for the Mexicans to find the condo, get at Najé, and kidnap Mrs. Gray. Their connections were incredible. How did they know their exact whereabouts? He and Julius had been careful when they'd gotten the condo. They had paid cash for the place for the exact reason of anonymity. Evidently their plan hadn't worked, and Devon was at a loss for words. "So, what do y'all expect us to do, Ma? We can't just rush into Dallas, guns blazing. Both of you girls are pregnant, and if anything happens to either one of you I'd hate myself forever," he said.

"I don't want to be away from you, Devon, and I know Angelica feels the same way about Julius, so you need to figure it out, babe, for real," Shayla said.

Julius looked into the night sky. It was pitch black, except for the stars that twinkled against the inky canvas. The moon, although a mere sliver, bounced pensively across the rippling water of the beach below.

He sighed heavily. His head hurt and he couldn't focus. He had lost so much in his young life, and he wasn't willing to put the people he loved most in any more danger. His Uncle Charlie, Aunt Pearl and his father had been killed in a war similar to this one, and it worried him.

Suddenly, it hit Julius like a ton of bricks. He whirled on his heels with a huge grin on his face. The two women and his brother stared at him in bewilderment.

"What are you grinning at, baby?" Angelica asked.

"I'm grinning because I have the perfect solution... *we* have the perfect solution. We've always had it right up under our noses," Julius said, knowing full well that everyone was on edge waiting for his big reveal.

"Spit it out, nigga!" Devon said, laughing.

"Okay, this is what I'm thinking. We still own the house in North Dallas. We could put Mama and the girls over there, and pay some of my niggas from the hood to do security at the crib. A bitch wouldn't get within ten feet of the crib without getting blasted!" Julius said triumphantly.

Najé appeared in the doorway and sashayed over to her son. "That's the best idea I've heard all night, baby. I'm all for it. Why don't I take the girls inside to start packing so that you boys can talk?" she said.

Devon and Julius nodded in agreement, and Najé

disappeared into the house with Angelica and Shayla in tow.

Devon was tired. He had left all his drama behind him in Detroit, and now he was in a whole new world, helping his brother deal with his own drama. The situation weighed heavily on his mind. In his profession, his targets were faceless to him. They were dollar signs, nothing more and nothing less. But this was different. There were people depending on him and Julius to make sound decisions and snap judgments. One false move could spell disaster for everything that they both held dear. "What's next, baby bro?" he asked.

"What do you mean, playa?"

"I mean, after all this shit is over, have you thought about what you're going to do?"

"After all what shit is over with?" Julius asked.

"Let me break it down for you. After we go to Dallas and take care of the Mexicans, what's your plan for the future, little brother?"

Julius dropped his head. With this madness going on, he really hadn't given it much thought. He and Angelica had made plans to move to Atlanta and that was still a viable option, but they had a lot to consider. They not only had the property in Dallas, but they also had the new condo in Miami to contend with. "On the real, Devon, I hadn't really given that much thought, know what I mean? All this shit going on really has me stressed out, dog. I just want my muhfuckin' life back. I wanna start fresh like I thought we were doing in Miami."

"Julius, I know you don't want to think about it right now, but you need to come up with a plan for the future. I'm sure this ain't what Dad had in store for his baby boy," Devon said sarcastically.

"What the fuck is that shit supposed to mean, nigga?" Julius had picked up on Devon's sarcasm and it struck a nerve. They had never spoken about the fact that Julius was raised by their father, while Devon wasn't. He was sure that his older brother had his share of animosity, but it was misplaced. Julius had nothing but love for his brother and their father, but he wouldn't stand by and bitch up for anybody.

"What I'm saying is that I'm sure Daddy didn't intend for me to be a fucking hit man, and I'm sure he didn't intend for you to be a career drug dealer and murderer."

Julius walked over to Devon and stood nose to nose with him. His eyes were searing holes into the eyes of his older brother. "Look out, playboy. Don't get it twisted. I got enough money to walk away from this shit right now. Ain't nobody tryna be no career drug dealer. You need to watch how you talk to me too!" he spat.

"Nigga, we're cut from the same cloth, so I hope you don't think you're puttin' no fear in my heart, *Junior!*" Devon countered.

Julius bumped Devon's forehead slightly with his

own. Devon in turn chest bumped Julius, but Julius stood firm. The brothers braced themselves for the inevitable, but just as suddenly as the aggression had arose, it was gone.

Devon's eyes softened, and Julius smiled. They both began to laugh. Silently, they wondered if their father and uncle had ever come to blows with one another.

"Man, this ain't for us, Ju. You're my baby brother and I love you, dog. We're gonna save that hatred for them niggas on the street. We're family, playa, and family holds family down, come rain or shine. I got your back 'til death, bro," Devon stated honestly.

Julius extended his hand, and Devon grabbed it and pulled him close. Julius' eyes said what his mouth was unable to. A single tear fell from his eye as he buried his head in his brother's shoulder.

Chapter 17

All About Us

Devon sat on the balcony, silently brooding. He and his little brother were so much alike that it was scary. True they had been cut from the same cloth, but he and Julius were two different breeds.

The stories that he'd heard as a child had been directly responsible for shaping and molding him into the man that he was today.

Julius had been raised by their father and their uncle, while he in turn had been raised by his mother and his father's two other brothers, Otha Lee and Eugene, who had been instrumental in turning Devon into an effective and lethal killer.

Growing up on the streets of Detroit had afforded Devon the opportunity to hone his skills, and today his brutality was not only legendary, but highly sought after. There were times when he would find himself wondering if there was something wrong with him, because he would sit and daydream about different ways to kill his prey.

The thing that made Devon so dangerous is that he had no conscience. He had often carried out his contract obligations late at night, and he would wake up the next morning as if nothing had happened, have a hardy breakfast and collect the remaining half of his bounty.

He had convinced himself that he was ridding the world of bad people, and although it was a weak justification for his actions, it seemed to appease the young man.

******

Devon's Uncle Eugene had shown up at his mother's funeral, unannounced. When Devon had noticed the man he had to do a double take. At a glance he was the exact duplicate of his father. "Do you know who I am, boy?" the raspy voiced man had barked.

"No... I mean, you kinda look like my father."

"I look *just* like your father. He's my brother. It's a Gage trait I suppose," Eugene said.

"So, why now? Why did you come around here all of a sudden? When me and my mama were struggling, nobody was there for us. You want to be family now, old man?" Devon snarled.

Eugene just stared at the young man and could see the hurt and pain in his eyes. It was strange to see his brother's seed without him being there. He didn't want to upset the boy, but he was a Gage, and they had work to do. When his brothers were killed, he'd gone into a deep depression and needed time to heal; time to grieve. And during that time he had lost numerous contracts in his "profession".

"I'm not trying to get into an arguing match with you at your mother's funeral, nephew. I need you to know that you have family here in Detroit, and it's our hope that you allow us to rally around you and hold you down," Eugene said.

As he watched his nephew, he could see the ruthlessness of Julius in his stance, but also the innocence of his little brother, Charlie Boy in his eyes. He handed his nephew a black business card with gold letters.

To Devon, the business card looked strange. It merely read: *GAGE 313-555-7426*. As he eyed the card he allowed his eyes to give the man the once over. He was dressed from head to toe in midnight black, from the suede fedora on his head to his black, big block alligator shoes. His suit, shirt and tie, and even his floor-length mink coat were black. The only hint of color were the gray streaks in his sideburns. He was impeccably dressed and he smelled like money.

"If you decide that you want to know your father's

side of the family, give me a call," Eugene said as he walked in the direction of a black Lincoln limousine.

This nigga's a limo driver. That's why he's dressed like that, Devon thought. But those thoughts were quickly put to rest when a sharply dressed young black man emerged from the driver's seat and scurried to the passenger's side to open the door for his uncle.

Eugene Gage looked over his shoulder in his nephew's direction and studied the young man's face, searching for something. His gaze was unsettling to the boy. He had managed to lock eyes with him but, Devon suddenly diverted his eyes. There was something in his uncle's eyes that frightened him... *death!* He had the eyes of a man that had seen too much of the wrong things.

Devon didn't realize it then, but Eugene had looked death in the face on too many occasions, and every time he faced death, it took a little bit more of his soul.

Devon wasn't sure if dialing his uncle's number had been a blessing or a curse.

His uncle had invited him to his lavish home in West Bloomfield. He didn't know that black people lived out there, let alone anyone in his family.

He pulled into the driveway in his beat up Honda Accord and parked. He rang the doorbell and waited. A boy close to his age answered the door and stared at him curiously.

"May I help you?" the boy asked.

"Yeah. I'm looking for Eugene Gage."

"You must be at the wrong address. This is the Miller residence," the boy said while still smiling.

Devon turned around to leave. He felt that it was probably too good to be true. Black folks didn't make money like that in Detroit unless they played sports.

"Hey!" the boy yelled just as Devon made his way back to his car. "I was just fucking with you, man. Eugene is my dad. He's inside. Come on in."

Devon returned to the house and pushed past the younger man. He wasn't particularly in a joking mood.

"Damn, man! Calm down! I'm your cousin, Demetrious."

"I'm Devon, bruh. I didn't mean any harm. I'm just tryna figure out what's going on."

"Follow me, Devon. I'll show you where everybody else is," Demetrious said.

As Devon followed his cousin through the house, he marveled at the sheer vastness of the space.

He stopped in the grandiose hallway to look at a painting that stretched from the floor to the ceiling. It was of four young boys surrounding a beautiful, dark skinned woman dressed in white Native American garb. The boys surrounding her were looking lovingly at the woman as she gazed out into the world from the painting. Her eyes sparkled, and her dark hued skin glowed in stark contrast to her regal wardrobe.

Demetrious noticed his cousin standing there

mesmerized by the painting, and joined him. "That's our grandmother, Gertrude. My dad had it painted some years back," he said.

"Where is she? She's really pretty. What is she; like Indian or something?"

"She's dead," Demetrious said solemnly. "Our grandfather killed her. My daddy said she was too pretty for him, and it drove the old man crazy with jealousy until he couldn't take it anymore." He shrugged.

As Devon turned to walk away he locked eyes with the woman in the painting. It was as though she was staring right at him, and into his soul. Her eyes seemed to follow him as he walked away, trailing closely behind his cousin.

Surprisingly enough, Devon felt at home. It was a feeling that he was not used to, especially since his mother had passed. He was open to hear any and everything that his uncle had to say concerning his father and family.

Devon was led out to an expansive backyard that seemed to stretch as far as the eye could see. As he and Demetrious made the trek across the yard towards a building at the edge of the property, the wind whistled and hissed around their heads indicating that snow would most definitely follow.

Devon hugged himself as he walked across the yard. His Member's Only jacket was far too thin for the encroaching winter wind. He could see the brick structure in the distance, and light snow flurries began to fall as they reached the doors.

The young men burst through the doors and were greeted by two very muscular black men with guns drawn.

"Demetrious, you need to make your presence known! You almost got popped!" one of the security guards said.

"Fool, this is *my* house! I ain't gotta make shit known!" he said as he slapped the man five. "This is my cousin, Devon," he announced while pointing over his shoulder.

The security guard gave Devon the "What's up" head nod.

Demetrious smiled at the man and asked him, "Aye where is everybody, Monsta?

Monsta was a thick necked, bald headed black man with muscles everywhere, even his earlobes. Devon noticed that his voice didn't fit his size. He had to be pushing at least 250-lbs, but he had the voice of a fourteen year old boy. His muscles rippled through his black turtleneck sweater. The shoulder holster that held his .45 caliber pistol seemed to barely fit over his massive deltoids.

"Follow me," Monsta said, and he led them towards a room with two huge doors made of African blackwood. He knocked on the colossal wooden door with the butt of his pistol, and it was answered by a young man that looked to be around Devon's age, maybe a little older.

The young man opened the doors to reveal a sizeable chamber. There was a fireplace on each side of the huge room, and the wood in the fireplace crackled and hissed as they entered. There were five other boys in the room, ranging in age from sixteen to twenty-one.

Devon saw the man that he had met at his mother's funeral, who had identified himself as his Uncle Eugene. He sat with another man who he guessed was probably also one of his uncles.

As he and Demetrius stepped into the room everyone stood.

"Welcome to the beginning of the rest of your life, young Devon. I'm your uncle, Otha Lee. Come, have a seat," the man instructed.

As Devon made his way over to his uncles, each one of his cousins was scrutinizing him closely.

"Greetings, nephew. I was elated when you phoned me. We have much to discuss, but first let me introduce you to your family," Eugene said. He walked around the room with Devon, introducing him to each of his six cousins.

After the introductions were made, his uncles requested that everyone have a seat.

Eugene began to speak first. "Nephew, what you see here is what is left of the Gage legacy. I'm not sure if anyone has told you, but you have a little brother in

Texas who was named after your father."

"Yeah, I know. My mom told me," Devon said.

His uncle nodded. He could hear the apprehension in his nephew's voice, and decided against going into detail about his little brother. Instead, he chose to give full attention to the area of bringing him into the "family business". Their business was a lucrative one built on death and destruction. The Gage family was virtually unknown to law enforcement, but revered in the underworld.

"Devon, we want to bring you into the fold; into the family business. It would probably be simpler to give you a wad of money and let you do your thing, but as the Bible says, 'Give a man a fish, and he will eat for a day. But if you teach him to fish, he can eat forever', and I believe that wholeheartedly. So, my young nephew, if you want to eat forever, we can show you how to make money," Eugene said nonchalantly.

Devon had the money that his father had left him in the safe, but he was intelligent enough to realize that the money he had wouldn't last forever. "What exactly is it that y'all do? What is the family business?" he asked.

Eugene looked at his brother and nodded.

Otha Lee waved his hands in the direction of his sons and nephews and began. "We have been able to train your cousins to be some of the most lethal and efficient killers that the world has ever known. The two easiest things in the world to do are to kill and to love.

We, on the other hand, love to kill. Do you see the irony in that statement?" he asked.

"You're telling me that you are a family of assassins?"

Eugene chimed in. "That's one way of putting it... yes. We are an advocate for the people that are unable to go to the police."

The thought of taking a life sent chills through Devon's body. He walked over to the fireplace and extended his hands, and rubbed them together vigorously. He stared into the flames as he thought about his mother and father. He was wishing that his life had somehow been different. He wasn't sure whether he was built for that kind of lifestyle, but this was his family.

His Uncle Eugene came over to him, tapped him on the shoulder and said, "Let me show you something, nephew." He motioned to Junior, the oldest of the sons and nephews.

Junior walked over to a large clock on the wall and moved the little hand to the four and the big hand to the nine. The wall that housed the fireplace where Devon had been standing slid open to reveal a room hidden deep within the recesses of the wall. Every person present except for security walked into the room.

On every available wall in glass cases were every gun imaginable. There were bows and arrows, crossbows, and even what appeared to Devon to be blow darts. There were so many ways to kill a man in the room that it made Devon dizzy.

On a large table in the center of the room were high quality photographs of what Devon surmised to be their marks.

The walls were made of aged stone, giving the room a cold, dismal feeling like a dungeon.

Devon walked around the room, taking in the full effect of his surroundings.

"This is where we keep our arsenal, nephew. Within this compound you'll learn to harm, kill and maim. You'll learn to disappear like a ghost before your target's body even falls to the ground. And, you'll learn to love it as every Gage man before you has, if you are willing to embrace your family heritage. Your father..." Otha Lee's voice trailed off as he looked away from his nephew while trying desperately to fight back his tears. "Your father was a great man, and although our profession seems a bit... well, a bit drastic to most, your father made us the best at what it is that we do," he said.

"Have you ever handled a gun, cuzz?" Tommy Lee asked.

"No, I can't say that I have," Devon replied.

"Alright, well, we'll change all of that."

From that day forward, Devon's life had revolved around the family business. His uncles enrolled him into the finest martial arts studios that money could buy. According to their philosophy, if you couldn't be far away enough to snipe a target, then you needed to be close enough to kill the mark with your bare hands.

There was a strict workout regimen. The boys were up by five a.m. every day to start their morning with an eight mile run. Then breakfast, weight lifting, martial arts training, and the gun range. The elder Gage men ran their young family members like an army boot camp.

It had been well worth it in Devon's eyes. He had become somewhat of a bad ass, and he relished in the fact that the average man could not compete with him when it came to fighting. He was also at the head of his class, so to speak, when it came to marksmanship. His accuracy was uncanny, and his uncles often remarked how he had the eyes of an eagle.

Now he would use those skills to help his brother out of this major dilemma. He had his father to thank for his killer instincts, and his uncles to thank for teaching him how to use those instincts and he would use every ounce of his being to keep his little brother safe.

Chapter 18

Julius' Revelation

Julius sat in the chair across from his bed, watching Angelica sleep. They had talked while he helped her finish packing. Angelica had made it painfully clear that his lifestyle wasn't what she wanted for their child, and he couldn't have agreed more.

Julius was at a loss. He didn't know what to do or where to turn. He had thought that he was doing the right thing by moving his family away from Dallas, but his chickens were indeed coming home to roost. He wanted and needed to close this chapter in his life. He thought that he had been thorough in dealing with his problems.

Detective McVey was on his way to prison, his old shady partner Sweeney was presumably dead, Rabbit was dead, and Julius' charge of capital murder for Booty Green's death had subsequently been dropped.

******

Yellow Shoes' fate depended on the outcome of Casper's appeal. If granted Julius would be content with letting Yellow Shoes spend the rest of his miserable life behind bars. But if the judge's decision was to deny Casper his freedom, the albino would murder Yellow Shoes. Julius in turn, would make certain to take care of his friend financially for the rest of his life.

All of Julius' bases were covered, with the exception of Flaco. He actually considered calling Mike Barrera to try and smooth things over and gain Mrs. Gray's freedom, but there was no way for him to know whether Mike was co-signing Flaco's behavior. Family was family, and Sleepy had died by *his* brother's hand. If the older Barrera was indeed in cahoots with his brother, then Julius had a lot to be worried about. If by chance he could understand what had gone down with Sleepy, Mike might be able to convince Flaco to back off.

It was well after 3 a.m., and he and his family had a 1 p.m. flight to New Orleans to catch. Julius was emotionally and physically drained, but he was too anxious to sleep. If he had his way, he would just as soon have the three ladies in his life take an extended vacation to anywhere that they wanted to go, versus going into the belly of the beast with him and Devon. He was intelligent enough to realize that he was walking into a potentially fatal situation, and he couldn't fathom the idea of anything happening to Najé, Shayla or Angelica.

Flaco had left Julius no choice in the matter. He would have to eliminate the threat, or die trying.

The worry of what might happen weighed heavy on his mind and heart, and before long Julius had drifted off to sleep.

Devon tapped lightly at Julius' door, but there was no answer. He cracked the door and peeked inside. The alarm clock on his nightstand read 8:30 a.m. Julius had fallen asleep in the chair across from his bed.

Devon walked over to Julius, knelt down next to him and shook him lightly.

Julius gave Devon a startled look, as if he was trying to figure out where he was.

"I need to talk to you, bro. Meet me in the living room," Devon said, and exited Julius bedroom.

Moments later, Julius walked into the living room, wiping the sleep from his eyes. "What's on your mind, bro?" he asked.

Devon looked into his brother's eyes. He wasn't sure if he would go for his plan, but he thought it through over and over again. "Man, I don't know what's been on your mind, but I hardly slept worth a damn last night. I tossed and turned, thinking about the best way to handle this shit, and basically, bruh, I came up with the fact that I'm not willing to leverage our family. We can't take the girls to Dallas with us; straight up," he said wearily.

Julius looked at his brother, laughed and shook his head.

"What's so funny, Ju?" Devon asked.

"Man, I know we're brothers, and I swear, dawg, that's exactly what I went to sleep thinking. I was like, if anything happens to either of them I'll never forgive myself."

"How the hell are we going to convince them to stay here though?" Devon asked. He knew that Shayla would never go for it.

"I'm thinking that if we give them about ten grand apiece, send them to Jamaica or the Bahamas and promise to keep them updated every day, they might just go for it."

"All we can do is try it, bro."

Najé came into the living room just as the boys were finishing their conversation. "All you can do is try what?" she asked as she headed straight over to the coffee pot. She needed her coffee to get her day started.

"I'd rather talk to all of the ladies in my life at one time, Mama, if that's okay," Julius answered.

Shayla and Angelica came out of their bedrooms at the same time, and entered the living room.

Angelica was truly everything that Julius could

have hoped for in a woman. "I won't drag this out. I'll keep it as simple as possible," he said before he disappeared into his bedroom.

Minutes later he re-emerged with a large stack of money and gave it to Angelica. "This is ten thousand dollars," he began. "This is enough money to go to the Bahamas or Jamaica and have a really good time. I want you ladies to take this money, and understand that you need to enjoy yourselves, wherever you choose to go; anywhere but, Dallas."

Shayla started to protest, but Devon silenced her with a wave of his hand. "Baby, this is non-negotiable. You three ladies will take this money and disappear until shit cools down. My daddy always said family first, and that's what this is."

Najé looked at Devon and Julius with a mixture of pride and apprehension. She was just getting to know Devon, but she knew without a shadow of a doubt that he would take care of her son with every ounce of his being. "Ladies, there is one thing I know, and two things for sure: Devon and Julius are products of their father, and if they think that it's best for us to be somewhere else besides Dallas, then I am willing to do that," she said. She knew as the matriarch of the family her word held weight. She had spoken, and her word was bond.

The Gage boys would enter Dallas alone and on their own. The only thing she could do was pray and put a veil of protection over her boys.

Chapter 19

The Unfriendly Ghost

Casper waited anxiously inside of the courtroom. His attorney was speaking with the district attorney and the judge as he watched nervously. His eyes darted around the room fretfully. The courtroom made him even more nervous, with its clinically white walls and wooden benches. It smelled of old cedar and cleaning solution and it was uncommonly cold. He shifted uncomfortably in his seat, trying to mentally prepare for what was to come.

There were a million things going through Casper's fragile mind. He had mental problems, and he was well aware of it. The thoughts that plagued his mind were sick and twisted visions of mutilation and doing bodily harm to other people. He had no idea what he would do. There was no fairytale ending or pot of gold at the end of his rainbow.

Casper had killed his immediate family, and had all but been disowned by the relatives who knew of his situation. They saw Casper as some sort of sick and perverted monster, and as thoughts of their fear rushed through his mind, his freckled lips twisted into a psychotic sneer.

As his attorney approached his table, Casper tried to interpret the man's facial features, but they were stoic; unreadable. "What's going on, man? What did they say?" Casper asked.

The lawyer didn't utter a word. He just looked into his client's eyes and shook his head.

Things didn't look promising, and Casper knew it. He wasn't even sure whether he *wanted* to go home because there was nothing to go home to.

The appellate court judge banged his gavel harshly against the wooden sound block. "This court will now come to order. I have heard arguments from both sides of counsel. Will the defendant please rise?" the judge ordered.

Casper stood slowly, scowling angrily at the judge. He had a sinking feeling in the pit of his stomach as the judge began to speak.

"Mr. Martin, you were tried as an adult by the State

of Texas, and as I read over your case, I wanted to believe that there had to be some miscarriage of justice. I wanted to believe that there was somehow some salvageable part of your young life. But, after closer examination, I believe that you knew exactly what you were doing. I believe that you are a calculating, cold blooded killer, and to let you go free would not only endanger the general public, but that in itself would be the greatest injustice of all."

"The sheer brutality of your crime is irrefutably the most heinous I have ever seen in my time on this bench. And to add insult to injury, you raped and killed your own sisters."

"It is with these facts that my judgment is that your sentence stands. You, Mr. Martin, are to be confined to the Texas Department of Corrections for a term of natural life. This is the order of this court, so sayeth the judge."

The Honorable Judge Larry W. Baraka banged his gavel once again, scooped up his bundle of files folders and headed back to his chambers.

Casper looked at his attorney. A small part of him was angry and aggravated, but a larger part was somewhat pleased with the judge's decision. There was nothing for Casper to worry about in prison. He was sure that they would more than likely send him to one of the older units; one of the "gladiator farms" that were mostly populated by young men under the age of twenty-five, and who loved to fight. Casper was good with his hands, and he was certain that his reputation would beat him to his next prison unit.

But before he was transferred to his unit, he had business to handle; family business.

It was well after six p.m. when Casper was finally transported back to his cell block.

Anxious jail guards at the end of their long event-filled day were changing shifts with other CO's that were meandering aimlessly toward their prospective destinations, while unruly inmates scurried about.

Casper sat on a nearby concrete bench with his ankles and wrists shackled to a heavy gauge metal ring bolted to the concrete floor beneath his plastic flip flops. His gazed was fixed on the bolt, but he wasn't looking at it. He was in some faraway place... a dark place.

He daydreamed of what method he would use to murder Yellow Shoes. He drifted deeper into the abyss of insanity. He contemplated pulling the blades from the cheap, indigent issued BIC razors, melting them into a toothbrush and then slashing Yellow Shoes' throat, but thought better of it because it would be too messy. The pimp would probably scream from the shock, drawing unwanted attention.

Casper's eyes darkened and his lips were twisted in a gruesomely grim smile. Spittle dribbled from his yellow teeth as his devious plan materialized in his psychotic mind. He was so deeply entrenched in his own twisted little world that he barely heard the guard speaking to him.

"Martin... Martin, get your thumb out of your ass and open your ears. Are you ready to go back to your cell?" the guard snapped.

"Yeah, I'm ready." He hated Miss Tolliver. She had been a pain in his ass ever since he came back on a bench warrant. She was a bull dike that hated all men, and it showed in every word that she spoke.

She knelt down to unlock his shackles, and in his mind he could see himself wrapping the chains around her thick, fat, hippopotamus-like neck and choking her until she shit on herself.

She grabbed his arm, snapping him out of his murderous fantasy, and nudged him slightly towards the direction of his cell block. When they arrived, the other CO's were in the middle of handing out dinner. Inmates were lined up at the bars in a single file line, impatiently waiting on their meager meal of bologna, stale bread, prunes, apple sauce and saccharin laced Kool-Aid.

Miss Tolliver unlocked the heavy metal-barred door with a twist of her over-sized skeleton key, and Casper walked onto the block with a cock sure swagger. His eyes searched feverishly for his prey. He spotted Yellow Shoes close to the back of the chow line, who waved the young psychopath over to join him.

"How'd it go, youngster?" Yellow Shoes asked eagerly.

Casper shrugged and said, "They banged me, man. They upheld the original conviction, so I'm here until I can appeal my shit again."

"Damn, that's fucked up, mane. Sorry to hear that," Yellow Shoes said. But in all actuality, he was glad that the boy would be sent back to prison. If they were sent to the same prison unit, he could surely use a strong young player like Casper to do his dirty work.

They ate dinner in relative silence, neither saying much. Both men were lost in their own thoughts. Yellow Shoes' thoughts were centered on how he could best utilize his young minion, while Casper's thoughts were more ominous. He needed to kill Yellow Shoes without getting caught.

"I think I'ma lay down for a minute, youngster. This garbage ass chow got my guts on twist," Yellow Shoes said, half groaning in pain.

"Do what you do, pimpin'. I'ma watch some of these Spanish ho's on *Telemundo*."

Yellow Shoes walked to his cell, and Casper knew that it would be just a matter of minutes before the old man was fast asleep. He would wait until the dayroom was bustling with activity and then make his move. But until the time came, he would watch the Spanish channel and fantasize about sexing one of the many luscious little Spanish girls that gyrated and twirled their hips seductively on the television.

Casper sat mesmerized as a young *chica* danced

slowly. Her ultra-short denim Daisy Duke shorts were cut just below her butt cheeks, her T-shirt had the Spanish slogan *"Jugoso"* printed across her chest, and the bottom of the shirt was cut off and barely hiding her supple breasts. As she twirled while lost in her own seductive world, her jet-black hair swooshed about her slender face. Her skin was tanned to perfection, and sparkled from the glitter-filled lotion and sunlight. He silently wondered where they were filming the TV show. Where on God's green earth could there be a place that had such a high concentration of gorgeous women? He wondered.

Casper looked around. There was nothing like a full stomach to get the inmates on the block moving around, no matter how harsh the menu.

Yellow Shoes' cellmate, Dirtbag noticed Casper fidgeting over his plate and seized the opportunity to beg. "Look out, homeboy. You gonna eat that?" he asked.

"Nah, handle your business, playboy. It's all yours."

Casper's hunger would be fed with blood. He moved slowly towards Yellow Shoes' cell while keeping a wary eye trained on the dayroom. At the top of the stairs he stopped and looked down the catwalk. He moved quietly down the run and stopped in front of his victim's cell.

Casper turned to face the large, open space. His dead, unfeeling eyes scanned the dayroom looking for any sign that he should abort his mission, but there were none.

He backed into Yellow Shoes' cell with his eyes still trained on the dayroom. Behind him he could hear the heavy labored breathing of his sleeping prey. He turned and moved quickly, straddling the old man and pinning his arms down with his knees.

Yellow Shoes was beyond startled. His eyes popped open and he opened his mouth to scream, but his scream was caught in his throat.

Casper clamped one of his baseball glove sized hands over Yellow Shoes' mouth and nose, and with the other hand he grasped his throat and squeezed tightly. Yellow Shoes wiggled and squirmed underneath the weight of the albino behemoth. "Do you know who I am?" Casper whispered.

Yellow Shoes' frantic, questioning eyes told him that he didn't.

"Today, I am the Grim Reaper!" he said, squeezing tighter. "Julius Gage wanted me to send his regards, muhfucka. He also says to kiss your boyfriend, Rabbit when you get to hell, punk." As Casper intensified his grip, he could hear the brittle bones of Yellow Shoes' windpipe cracking as he applied maximum pressure.

The old pimp had held his breath as long as he possibly could in hopes that this was his young friend's idea of a twisted prank.

Then, his movements ceased altogether. He was

unable to fight off the inevitable any longer. He felt as if he were drifting into a deep sleep of which he had no control.

It was true what they said. You *do* see your whole life flash before your eyes in your final moments. A tidal wave of memories came rushing back at the pimp;

He could see his mother standing at the kitchen sink, peeling potatoes in her favorite flower patterned dress. He could hear his father humming church hymns as he tended the garden that ran along the side of their modest, wood framed farm house in Crockett, Texas. He could feel the sunshine beaming on his face, and hear the raucous laughter of his grandfather as he rode in his lap on the tractor through the orange groves in Haines City, Florida.

Yellow Shoes blinked away a single tear, and he could see Julius and Charlie Gage in the distance of a long black tunnel, taunting him, and beckoning for him to join them.

Suddenly, there were no more memories. Death slammed his eyes shut and welcomed him as his body gave one final jerk.

Casper felt the tension in Yellow Shoes' body subside and loosened his grip. He removed his hand from his mouth and nose and climbed off of him. He leaned down next to him and felt for a pulse, but there wasn't one. He opened Yellow Shoes' mouth and listened for a breath of life, but the breath never came.

Satisfied that Yellow Shoes was dead, Casper turned him over onto his side and positioned his body to look as though he were sleeping. He put his hands together and stuck them underneath his head, bent both of his knees, and cocked one slightly more than the other to give a rested appearance. He then smiled to himself. Yellow Shoes looked like a small child sleeping peacefully.

Casper stood up and exited the cell. The inmates on the block were still busy with their chosen activities.

He made his way down the catwalk to his cell three doors down from where Yellow Shoes lay dead. He stretched out on his bunk and folded his hands neatly behind his head and stared at the under-side of the top bunk.

It would be count time soon, and everyone would be required to return to their cells. As soon as they un-racked in the morning, he would place a call letting someone know that the "business" had been handled.

"Count time! Count time! Rack it up, fellas!" came the call over the loud speaker.

Casper turned over onto his side and stared blankly at the wall. He waited to hear Dirtbag's panicked scream as inmate after inmate shuffled past his cell on their way to their own confined spaces. He heard the sound of the bars sliding shut, the loud rattling of gears echoing against the stone walls and stopping suddenly with a loud thud.

Miss Tolliver lumbered down the catwalk counting slowly. She passed Yellow Shoes' cell and continued towards where Casper lay resting. When she reached his cell she stopped, peeked inside and jotted something down on her clipboard. "Martin, roll it up. You're on the chain. You're headed to Coffield Unit, tough guy," she said.

Casper didn't say a word. He jumped up from his bunk, grabbed his commissary bag and tossed his meager belongings inside. He looked at Miss Tolliver with murder in his eyes as he lay back down.

Something in his eyes struck fear in the young lesbian. "You got one collect call before you catch the chain. You can call as soon as I'm done with count time, okay?" she said sweetly.

Casper smiled to himself. He had never once heard her utter a kind word to anyone, but all of a sudden she was nice as hell. "Yeah, that's cool. I need to let somebody know I'm being shipped," he said.

Tolliver scurried off to finish her count, and later returned to escort Casper to the payphones. "When you're done, just re-rack and I'll close and lock your cell from the picket. Take your time," she said in a syrupy tone of voice.

Casper walked to the payphone and dialed the number. Seconds later, Duddy answered the phone. "Hello?"

"What it was, cuzz?" Casper responded.

"What it was, cuzz? Who this?"

"Yo, it's Casper, folk. Tell big homie, Ju that I

shined my shoes and I'm headed to Coffield. They sending me to the gladiator farm," Casper informed, and then hung up the phone. He knew he'd done well, and that Julius would be proud.

Everything would change tomorrow though. He would be headed to the Coffield Unit; the place that nightmares were born.

Chapter 20

This Ain't Livin'

Julius and Devon had made it safely into Dallas with their cargo van full of weapons. Shayla had done as she'd promised, and every detail was on point. The weapons had been preloaded, and the van was waiting in the parking garage of the Louis Armstrong Airport in New Orleans. They had driven to Dallas on pins and needles, because crossing state lines with weapons was automatic Fed time, and neither man wanted to face those consequences.

The Adolphus Hotel was one of the most prestigious hotels in Dallas. Julius and Devon sat in a plush suite on the top floor overlooking the skyline of downtown Dallas, contemplating their next move. Devon had convinced Julius to reach out to Mike Barrera. As he explained, they at least needed to gauge his reaction to the phone call, which would give them an idea as to his position on the situation.

Julius had reluctantly agreed. He sat on the side of the plush hotel room bed, staring at the phone. *Here goes nothing,* he thought. He picked up the phone and dialed the number.

"This is Mike. Speak on it."

"M.B., what's up, mane?" Julius said.

"J.G., what's going on, *chabalito?*"

"*Nada.* Listen, I have a problem."

"Yes, *vato.* We have a mutual problem."

"Oh yeah? How so?" Julius asked curiously.

"Flaco is operating blindly, and his actions are unpredictable. His hatred for you and your brother threatens to derail all that I have worked to accomplish. I refuse to lose, J.G."

"Yeah, *jefe.* I can understand that, but have you given any thought as to how we can rectify this situation?"

"I have some ideas of which I do not wish to speak of on the telephone. How about you meet me somewhere?"

"Remember that place where all of the young gangsters used to hang out on the south side, on 2nd Avenue?"

"Yes, I remember."

"Meet us there at ten p.m."

Mike agreed, and hung up the phone.

Julius replaced the receiver on his end and turned to his brother. "Well, bro, it's done. Now let's just hope and pray that this muhfucka don't try no slick shit."

"So, what did he say?" Devon asked.

"I'll explain on the way to the south side. I want to get there early and make sure we're not being set up."

As they drove, Julius explained to his brother all of the things that Mr. Barrera had shared with him, especially how he saw Flaco as a threat to both sides.

Devon and Julius pulled into the dimly lit parking lot of the Lady Pearl Pool Hall and parked in the back, facing the alley. They backed the van up against the back of the building so that there was no chance for anyone to come through the back door. Besides, the brothers wanted a fast and clean getaway if the situation got serious.

The parking lot was empty except for an overfilled trash dumpster and a red, beat up pickup truck. It was nine forty-five p.m., and Mike Barrera should be arriving soon.

Devon climbed into the back of the van and opened two aluminum crates. After examining the contents he reached inside and handed Julius two chrome .45 caliber pistols, and for himself he chose two .40 caliber handguns. "Let's go inside and post up, bro," he said to

Julius.

They exited the van and headed around the building towards the front door.

Along the way they passed an elderly black man in tattered overalls, standing at the back of the raggedy pickup truck. Julius gave the man a once over from head to toe, and nodded a quick "What's up" in his direction. But when he locked eyes with the man, there was something familiar about him. Julius also noticed that the man's shoes were too clean for the clothes that he had on and the truck he drove, but he shrugged it off as coincidence.

Devon and Julius entered the smoke-filled pool hall side by side. If they were going out, they were going out together with guns blazing. A Millie Jackson tune wafted dreamily through the air from the jukebox. "*...No pain, no pain, no gain, no gain...,*" she crooned.

There were very few people in the bar from what the brothers could see. An older couple hugged and fondled one another while they played pool. A couple of younger men sat in a booth close to the back of the lounge in deep conversation.

Devon and Julius walked to the bar and took a seat, and the bartender asked, "What will it be, fellas?"

Devon looked at the man who never looked up. He just kept wiping the bar with the dingy white rag. "I don't think that I have my ID with me, so I guess we'll both just have a coke," he said.

"We sell two kinds of coke here, boy; the kind that goes in your nose, and the kind you use to chase liquor. Money is the only ID you need here at Lady Pearl's boy. So like I said, what will it be?" the bartender hissed.

"In that case, give us a couple of Hennessey's and cokes, and bring the bottle to that table in the corner," Devon said.

They sat in the furthest corner of the smoky tavern, watching the front door intently.

Devon took a few deliberate drags from his Newport, tilted his head back and blew smoke rings toward the ceiling. He exhaled inaudible sounds of impatience and frustration. "Fuck this dude at, man? It's after ten," he said impatiently.

"Chill out, Devon. He'll be here, bro."

The old man that they'd seen in the parking lot walked in. His eyes scanned the lounge warily, as if he was looking for something or someone. He went to the bar, ordered a drink and headed towards the brothers. When he reached their table, Devon and Julius looked up at the old bum who was standing there motionless staring at them.

"What's up, old school? Are you lost?" Julius asked.

The old man didn't utter a word. He just sat down across from them, still staring.

"Bruh, what the fuck is up? You need to try and find somewhere to be and something else to focus on,"

Devon told him.

"You got some spare change, mister? I can shine ya shoes or wash that nice van y'all got out there?" Then, the old man threw his head back and laughed, revealing straight, white, evenly spaced teeth. "Julius, Devon it's me, Mike, man!" he said, and laughed some more.

Devon and Julius looked at the man closely, squinting in the low light trying to see his face. Then they all laughed.

"I'll be a muhfucka! Damn, it *is* you, Mr. B! What's with the disguise, man?" Julius asked.

"You can never be too careful. Flaco has eyes and ears everywhere. I just took the necessary precautions to make sure that we're all safe," Mike said.

"So, let's cut to the chase, Mr. B. What do you have in mind?" Devon asked.

"Listen, I know my brother. He functions from what he can see and what he feels, more than functioning from rationality. I, on the other hand, function on rational thinking. I think I came up with a viable solution to this whole ordeal. Your uncles are hit men, but my brother doesn't know about them. I can tell him that I'm hiring some outside shooters to eliminate our problem. If he goes for it, we hire your uncles and we go full Hollywood, with splattering blood packs and everything. You boys plan on leaving for Atlanta, Miami or wherever you're going anyway, so it's not like he'll see you milling around town. If he was anyone else, there would be no doubt as to how I would handle it. But he is my brother, so this will have to do," Mike explained.

"That's all fine and dandy, but I haven't even contacted my uncles yet to let them know what's going on. Knowing them the way that I do, they would just as well kill your brother than to put on some type of Hollywood production, Mr. B.," Devon said.

"Your uncles will go for it as long as you two are willing. As they say in the ghetto, my young friend, 'Money talks and bullshit walks. I have already put the plan into motion, so all you two have to do is be where I tell you, when I tell."

Mike stood up to leave, and Julius stood with him. "Mr. Barrera, I appreciate all that you're trying to do, but I need to find Angelica's mother. And your brother tried to have my mother murdered so I need you to understand that if I encounter Flaco while I'm handling my business—"

Mike stopped Julius short of finishing his sentence with a wave of his hand. "I was unaware that Flaco acted against your mother and let me worry about Mrs. Gray, Julius. She will leave with you boys when the time comes. Trust me."

Chapter 21

La Familia

Mike Barrera was livid. He paced his ample office space with his hands tucked deeply into the pockets of his white Armani slacks. There was too much betrayal and deceit going on for him to concentrate on business.

Flaco had mercilessly gone to their sister, Carmelita and told her that they'd found the men responsible for her son's murder. Flaco had also thought it necessary to inform her with an impish grin on his face that their oldest brother, the patriarch of their family, was refusing to give the green light to avenge her son's murder.

Carmelita had been grief stricken, falling to the floor in a fit of rage and sadness. Her piercing screams had drawn Mike from his perch next to the infinity pool in his backyard. He'd gone inside only to see his baby sister on her knees and crying uncontrollably. She cried and muttered profane obscenities in Spanish about how Mike was just as evil as the men that had murdered her son.

Mike knelt next to Carmelita to comfort her, but she jerked away violently. She was inconsolable.

Flaco leaned against the wall and watched the spectacle unfold.

"Flaco, what is wrong with Lita?" Mike asked. He was confused by her reaction to his touch. She was the youngest of the three siblings, and their relationship had always been solid.

"I was honest with her; something that you seem to know nothing about these days, brother."

"What have I not been honest about, *mi hermano?*"

"You *are* protecting our nephews killers, are you not?" Flaco asked sarcastically.

"*Tonto pendejo, Flaco!* My office, *now!*" Mike screamed.

That had been an hour ago, and Flaco still hadn't come to Mike's office. As he waited, it donned on him that he had been playing checkers, and his little brother had been playing chess.

Flaco was trying to force his hand and back Mike into a corner in hopes that Mike would make the moves that Flaco wanted him to make.

Mike reached into his cedar humidor and pulled out a fresh Cohiba, and took a long whiff of the sweet smelling, bourbon dipped tobacco. He bit the tip off of it and spit it into a marble ashtray. Carmelita hated for him to smoke in the house, but he needed it to calm his nerves.

Carmelita tapped lightly at the door and entered uninvited, followed closely by Flaco. They entered the office with their heads down, staring at the floor. They looked like the same small children whom he'd disciplined and scolded in their younger years, and now as adults they stood before him with their eyes cast downward as if ashamed to meet their brother's piercing gaze.

"To what do I owe the pleasure of the company of both *mi hermano y hermano*?" Mike asked.

"*Vato*, Lita has something that she wants to say to you," Flaco answered.

"Mikey, I am not sure why you chose to not pursue the men that murdered my son—your nephew—but it breaks my heart. When Sleepy's father was murdered you spared no expense to avenge his death. I guess that was different, because he made you millions of dollars right, *panzòn*? Sleepy was your *sobrino*! He loved you and looked up to you! Don't let my son's death go unanswered for. Please, Mike! I am begging, *jefe*. Please!" Carmelita said. Weeping, she dropped to her knees and continued to beg. "Please, Mikey. He was my *niño*; my only child!"

Mike reached down to help his sister up off of the floor. "Stand up, Carmelita. There is no need to beg. You are absolutely right, my love. He was my *sobrino*, and the men responsible will be punished. You have my word. Now leave us. I need to speak with Flaco." He kissed her on the forehead and walked her to the door. When she was out of sight Mike, turned to Flaco. "What the fuck is wrong with you, *panzòn?*" he shouted.

Flaco walked to the bar in the corner of the large office, looked over his shoulder and smiled at his brother. He took two small glasses from a cabinet and filled them with tequila. He extended a glass to his brother and said, "Mike, listen. Maybe I was wrong for telling Lita, but I needed you to see things from our point of view. You see everything through green lenses, meaning you arrange things in order of importance by their monetary value. Lita and I, on the other hand, see the most important thing as family." Flaco then took a swig from the expensive tequila.

"Is that what you believe, *chabalito?* You think that I put money above all else?"

"Well, you utilized a lot of our *soldados* and tens of thousands of dollars in order to punish the men that killed Smiley, and you didn't even like that *puto*. You never thought he was good enough for Lita, but her heartache caused you to spend countless *pesos* to avenge his death, and do you know why? Because he made us plenty of *pinché dinero*, that's why!"

Flaco had Mike against the ropes and he knew it, so he pressed on. "What does it matter to you if we eliminate a couple of *chongos*? He is no longer directly making the family money anyway," he said dismissively.

"And what do you propose we do with the girl's mother, with whom you have been having relations with regularly? Or did you think that I wouldn't find out?"

"We can either kill her or let her go. It makes no difference to me. She has fallen in love, *mi hermano*, so if we let her go, she will never snitch," Flaco said proudly. He was very aware of his prowess with women, and for years he had used it to his advantage.

But Veronica Gray was different for him though. He had never been in love before or had even given it a second thought. In his business women were plentiful. Beautiful women came and went for the graying man.

Veronica was beautiful, intelligent and insatiable. Her sexual hunger was beyond satisfaction. She was a freak in bed, and Flaco had taken her from the warehouse and put her in a small apartment close to the Barrera compound. He kept the place heavily guarded so there was no chance of her leaving. She was still held captive by all accounts, but it made their sexual trysts much more comfortable.

He had told his brother that if it came down to it, he would be willing to either kill her or let her go, but deep down inside he didn't want to do either. She had his nose wide open and she knew it. Flaco was allowing himself to fall deeper under Veronica's spell and he liked it… to a certain extent.

"So Mike, how do you propose we handle this situation? I mean, if I had my way we would just go to Miami and blast the *pendejos* and kill everybody," Flaco snorted.

"Let me handle that, brother. Julius and Devon come from a long line of killers, and if we do that, we will have to eliminate the Gage bloodline totally, or we'll forever be watching our backs."

"Okay, so again; what is the plan?"

"I already have Julius and his brother convinced that we want to have a sit-down with them. I also have been in contact with their uncles. Listen and learn, baby brother."

Mike then pulled a number from his desk and dialed. "Hello, may I speak with Eugene, please? Yes Eugene, this is Mike Barrera, and I have a solution to our problem. I have convinced my brother to have a sit-down with your nephews, and I would like for the rest of the Gage men there for balance. Let's say eight o'clock tomorrow night?" After a confirmation from Eugene, Mike replaced the receiver and smiled at his brother.

If things went according to plan, then the Gage's would be extinct, and he and his brother could get back to doing what they did best; making money. "I am proud of you, Mike. I know that you had reservations about this, but I believe that it is for the best," Flaco said. He gulped the remaining tequila and left the office.

Mike was confident in his role as a gangster, but he was more of a businessman. Nevertheless, he was intelligent enough to realize that trying to cross the Gage's was a risky endeavor.

He went to his safe and removed a manila envelope and examined the contents. In the envelope was the embodiment of a contradiction of the man that he had become. He had lived his whole life believing in just the opposite of what the envelope held, but he had no choice. Inside the envelope was evidence of the Gage family's hits. They were records that Mike had paid a pretty penny to obtain. If anything happened to him he would leave instructions for Carmelita to go to the authorities. He sighed heavily. This situation was surreal.

Mike took the short trek to Carmelita's bedroom and knocked on her door. There was no answer, so he went inside and placed the envelope in the top dresser drawer across from her bed. Then he sat at her vanity table and scribbled a quick note:

My dearest Carmelita;

You are my life, my world, and I love you, little sister. Anything you have ever asked of me I have given freely, and this situation is no different.

Sometimes in life it takes a slap in the face to help us see the things that should have been clearly visible in the first place. I am going to rectify this situation, my love. I also want you to know that I have never been afraid of anything in my life, but this scares me. If anything happens to me, I want you to take the manila envelope that I left in your top drawer straight to the police.

I love you always with every ounce of me.

Mikey

Mike placed the letter behind a picture attached to the mirror where he knew that she would find it. It was behind a picture of Mike, Flaco, and Carmelita holding Sleepy when he was just weeks old. He knew that she would see the note because she stared at the picture everyday as a reminder of good times gone by.

Mike's mind drifted to Miss Guerra. He was certain that this was not what she had in mind for her adopted grandson. Miss Guerra had always cautioned Mike to beware of trouble, but he had allowed greed to pull him into a world of which there could possibly be no return.

He felt a cold chill and shivered. An old saying crept into his head: *When you experience a cold chill, it meant that someone was walking across your grave.*

His heart was heavy with worry. The Gages were a dangerous family, and as mild-mannered as Julius came across, he was just as deadly as the lineage that he was born from. Any other time going into a situation of this magnitude, Mike was all *machismo*. But this was different; he *felt* different.

He decided to retreat to his bedroom, have a stiff shot of tequila, smoke a Cohiba and call it a night.

Chapter 22

Mi Hermana's Aflicción

Flaco greeted the guards who were keeping watch over his mistress's apartment. It was tucked away nicely on the fifth floor. It had no balcony and no means of escape.

During one of their many sexual rendezvous, Veronica had passionately whispered in Flaco's ear that she had fallen in love with him. But she refused to be held captive in a warehouse. She haughtily informed him that the least he could do if he planned to hold her captive is make the accommodations bearable. Flaco had hastily agreed, seeing as though he wanted a place to have her to himself.

He walked into the small, but inviting apartment and found Veronica lounging seductively on a plush, micro fiber suede couch. She was dressed as if she were expecting him, in a red lace baby-doll nighty, red stilettos and red crotch-less panties. She had requested that Flaco send one of his goons to do some shopping for her, since she wasn't allowed to leave the apartment. "You look gorgeous, my love... good enough to eat!" Flaco teased.

Veronica eyed her Latin lover seductively. "You know what I find really strange?" she asked.

"What is that, *mi amor?*"

"I think I'm suffering from 'Stockholm syndrome'," she said with a laugh.

"And just what is this Stockholm syndrome, Teacher?"

"It's a sickness of the mind that makes a victim fall in love with her captor. You did kidnap me after all," she said.

For a second he didn't say a word. Then he touched his index finger to her cheek. "It's not Stockholm syndrome, luscious, it's this," he said, and pointed to his tongue.

Veronica's breath caught in her throat as he traced his fingers to her breasts, then her stomach, until he finally reached the hem of her nighty. He slipped his finger ever so slightly between her legs. "Say stop whenever you want me to," he whispered.

Instead of stopping him, she opened her knees

slightly. He slid his entire hand between her legs and grazed her clitoris through her underwear. She moaned, and Flaco pressed his lips firmly against hers, bringing her moans to silence.

He slipped his thumbs through the lace strings on her panties and pulled them off. "Lie back and relax," he said.

She took a deep, shaky breath and obeyed.

He cupped the underside of her thighs to hook her legs over his shoulders before kneeling down. She gasped when she felt the warmth of his tongue between her legs. Flaco traced a small circle ever so softly around her clitoris. Gradually he increased his pressure and pace.

Veronica came hard, spraying a hot, wet milky mist across his chin.

Flaco stood up, unbuckled his belt and stepped out of his pants and boxers. His erection was pointing straight out, thick and hard. "Stand up, baby." he said.

Veronica did as she was told as he put his hands on her shoulders and turned her around.

"Don't move." He bent her over at the waist and entered her slowly.

"Oh my God!" she gasped. He pumped into her slowly, and with every thrust her clit rubbed against the suede couch. "Deeper!" she pleaded, arching her back and pushing her ass back, trying to take all of him inside of her.

Flaco grabbed her hair and pulled it so hard that her head tilted back, as he thrust himself deep up inside of her. "Is this what you want, *mi amor*? Is this how you like it?" he gasped.

"Yes! Oh my, God yes!" she cried out, feeling as though she was losing all control.

Flaco thrust into her deeply and grit his teeth as he rolled his hips back and forth, filling her and slamming her against the couch. He pounded into her so hard that it hurt, and she welcomed the pain. He came loudly, throwing his body over hers, his chest pressed firmly against her bare back. He was panting wildly and sweating profusely.

Flaco rolled off of Veronica and sat on the couch. Veronica grabbed his hand. He reluctantly stood up and she led him to the bathroom and started the shower. They stepped into the shower, and she washed his entire body with slow, sensual, soapy circles, making Flaco want to make love to her all over again.

She traced the soapy towel down his chiseled chest to his erect manhood, rinsed it under the warm water and dropped to her knees, taking him into her mouth.

Flaco leaned back against the cold tile and groaned in pleasure as he watched the steaming water cascade over Veronica's head. She ran her tongue in a circular motion around the head of his penis. He reached down and picked her up. "You know that I love you, right, *mi amor?*" he said.

Veronica looked searchingly into Flaco's eyes. She was old enough to know that a man didn't ask those types of questions without motive or reason. "Yes, I know that—I mean, I *feel* that. Why do you ask, *papi*?"

The last thing that Flaco wanted to do was lose Veronica, but she had served her purpose. It was time to release her and let her go home to her family. "My love, I am releasing you tomorrow. My brother and I have a meeting with your future son-in-law, his brother and their uncles. It is my intention to let you leave with those young men," he said.

Veronica had a mixture of emotions rushing through her head. She had originally seduced Flaco to get out of the warehouse and to fulfill her sexual cravings, but in the midst of it all she had fallen in love with the man. She knew that if she continued to see him, Angelica and Julius would never understand. Angelica would be a new mother in a few months, and she knew that her daughter would need her. Flaco had her intoxicated though; almost dick-drunk. "What if I say that I don't want to go? Are you going to *make* me leave?" she asked.

"I can't *make* you do anything. But your daughter is pregnant. Besides, you don't want to live the life I lead. Death is around every corner, Ronnie. If something were to happen to you, I would never forgive myself," he said, reaching for a towel and stepping out of the shower.

Veronica wanted to go to her daughter, truly she

did, but she was also desperate to keep that magical thing between Flaco's legs planted deep within her. Inwardly, she seethed, her blood almost reaching a feverish boil. She felt dejected, almost betrayed in a sense. She had given this man a part of her soul, made love to him and shared not only her body but her hopes and dreams as well.

"Flaco—and I understand your concerns, but—you have to realize that I am a big girl. I didn't come into this situation with blinders on. I came into this with no expectations or forethought. I dove in head first—better yet heart first—and now you're standing here telling me that it's over; telling me that I was just a piece of pussy to you?" she fumed.

"Are those the words that I used, my love? No, they are not. I am merely stating the obvious. Your son-in-law will never let you and I be together. There is too much bad blood."

"So, where do we go from here?" she asked sincerely.

"I suggest we take it one day at a time, *mi amor*. I have never been anyone's secret, but for you I am willing to make that concession." Flaco felt guilty for lying to her. She would most likely perish along with her daughter's precious Julius. He liked her a lot, but business was business.

He knew his brother, and if Mike resolved to eliminate the problem, then he would most definitely do his part. He would have his soldiers in place to assassinate the Gage's as soon as they exited the busy restaurant of the Adolphus Hotel. There would be plenty of witnesses so that it would be a deterrent for trouble inside the restaurant.

Flaco smiled to himself. Only a miracle would save the men. He wanted them all dead, and the sooner the better.

Veronica noticed the sly smirk on Flaco's face and decided against asking him what he was thinking about. In her mind he would probably just lie anyway. She was nobody's fool. Flaco had his hidden agendas, and so did she. Although she had dropped her defenses and allowed herself to catch feelings for the man, initially it had all been about survival. Self-preservation was the key. With the exception of Angelica and the countless third graders that she taught, Veronica had always been about self. She would do as Flaco said, and let the scenario play itself out.

In the words of her mother: "If you have no expectations, you'll have no disappointments." *Amen to that, Mama! Amen to that!* she thought.

Chapter 23

A Change Gonna Come

Julius looked so much like their father that his uncles had both stopped in their tracks and stared at him for a long while when he'd answered the door to the hotel room. "Jesus Christ, boy! You even sound like yo' damn daddy, voice and all." Otha Lee had said upon meeting their nephew for the first time. Now, Eugene paced back and forth in the luxurious hotel room. He was anxious, but then again he was always anxious before a hit. This was different though. The Mexican, Mike Barrera had changed the plans more than once, and it was unsettling. There were reasons for everything, and Eugene would make damn certain that those reasons didn't creep up and bite him on his blind side. The phone call from Devon informing them of what their plans were had made him wonder if the Mexican was being on the up and up. Devon wanted them to meet Julius and get a feel for the situation before this "meeting" even took place.

"Damn, Unc! You're going to wear a hole in the carpet with ya nervous ass, why are you pacing like that?" Julius asked jokingly.

Devon looked at his uncle, and then at his brother. He loved the fact that his brother and uncle had hit it off instantly.

"On the real though, before we go into this situation let me ask y'all something." Julius said.

"What's that nephew?" Otha Lee asked.

Julius sat for what seemed like an eternity before speaking. Julius' voice cracked slightly as he choked back tears. "Where were y'all when I needed you? Daddy and Uncle Charlie were murdered and neither one of you even bothered to come to the funeral. I mean y'all rallied around Devon after his Mom passed but, our Dad was your brother and y'all left me hanging." He said. Eugene tried to speak but Julius cut him off, "hold up let me finish, why didn't you at least let me know that I had family instead of making me feel like it was just me and Ma?" He said between tears. Eugene moved in next to his nephew and put his arm around him.

"Julius Jr. I fucked up, hell we fucked up and I'm

sorry. This shit is crazy, we are just meeting for the first time in your short eighteen years and I feel that I owe you an explanation. Ju when your Daddy died it sent me into a downward spiral, your Pops had always been more of a father to us than a brother and I couldn't bear the pain of seeing him in no casket. You were young and impressionable but, you had your mother to care for you. I'm sorry nephew; I have no excuses to offer." Eugene said.

"But why didn't y'all get revenge against them Unc? That nigga married my Mama like he was taunting me!!" Julius screamed. It killed Otha Lee inside to see his young nephew so distraught. He kneeled in front of Julius and looked him in the eyes.

"Julius would you believe me, if I said that your father knew that he was going to die and asked us not to seek revenge?" His concern wasn't with vengeance; his concern was making sure that you boys knew each other; that you learned to love one another even under the circumstances. We dropped the ball on that one but, your father didn't want us to hunt his killers down. We are your uncles yes but, ultimately when all is said and done Devon is your brother and you two are all you have in this world." Otha Lee said.

"Ok mane, I will grant y'all that," Julius said feeling better, "but my original question still stands, why you pacing and shit?" he said laughing.

"I'm pacing because I don't trust them bean eatin'

muthafuckas, nephew," Eugene spat.

"Yeah, me either," offered Otha Lee. "We are going to hafta be on our P's and Q's dealing with those dudes, man. I wish we would've brought the boys," he said, referring to their sons.

"Those cats say that they want peace, so maybe everything is everything," Devon said and shrugged.

"You know, nephew, for you to be so smart, mane, sometimes I worry about you," Eugene laughed.

"Why? What made you say that, Unc?"

"He said that because he's a man just like you, and you never underestimate another man, bro. I'm the youngest. Hell, you should be teaching me that, old ass dude!" Julius said and playfully punched his brother.

"Eugene, I swear this little fucker is his daddy reincarnated. I don't know how Julius Sr. managed to have two sons who each got an equal part of his personality, but I'll be damned if that nigga didn't!" Otha Lee said.

There was an eerie silence that filled the room. The meaning wasn't lost on anyone present. It seemed that Julius Sr.'s presence could be felt all around them.

"Yeah, he did do that shit. If he was here right now we wouldn't be having this conversation, or be in this situation. Julius would have eliminated the threat before it became a threat. I swear, that black ass nigga had a sixth sense when it came to danger," Eugene laughed.

"Well, I got a sixth sense too, and my sixth sense is

telling me not to trust them either. I'm sure they're coming strapped, so best believe I'll have my burner close," Julius said.

"Straight up, baby bro, I second that notion," Devon agreed.

The men sat around the living room of the hotel suite and formulated their plans. They would go to the restaurant first thing in the morning and have breakfast so as to not look suspicious, but paying careful attention to every detail.

Julius would walk the kitchen to map out an exit route if it came down to it.

Devon would walk the front of the building to get a feel for the surrounding area.

After breakfast they would all walk the back alleys and scope out the most accessible escape routes. Proper preparation was essential for making the meeting a success.

"Y'all little gangsters need to get some sleep. We have a long day ahead of us tomorrow," Eugene said.

The uncles exited the boys' room and headed across the hall to their own room.

The following day would be a trying time for the family.

Devon sat at the edge of the bed, staring at his brother but not really looking at him.

"What's on your mind, Devon, man? You have that faraway look in your eyes," Julius said.

Julius' voice brought Devon out of his daydream. "I'm just thinking about Shayla, bro. In my business I've erased a lot of people in my short lifetime, but those were hits and always at a distance. This is different. We are going face to face with the enemy, and it scares me, Julius. I finally fell in love, and I don't think it's fair to Shayla that I'm still out here doing wrong while she's pregnant, you know?"

Julius looked at his brother and began to laugh hysterically. The laughter was so loud and obnoxious that it startled Devon.

"What's so damn funny, man?" Devon asked.

"I'm laughing because you sound like a little bitch right now, nigga. My girl is pregnant too, but I'm not trippin' on that shit. Love will get your ass killed out here. So, I put that at the back of my mind and concentrate on handling my business," Julius said, suddenly all business.

Devon knew from the look in his younger brother's eyes that he was serious, and the topic wasn't up for debate.

******

Across the hall from the young brothers, the uncles huddled in a corner, talking late into the night.

Eugene and Otha Lee Gage had been absent for most of Devon's life, and for all of Julius' life. They both felt somewhat guilty for what they saw as abandoning their nephews.

When Julius Sr. and Charlie Boy had been murdered, they both had been plagued with bouts of guilt. The fact that they hadn't gone to Dallas and eliminated Yellow Shoes, Rabbit and Booty Green had always made the brothers feel cowardly. But Julius Sr. had penned an ominous letter to the brother's weeks before his murder, instructing them to not act if anything happened to him. He said that his life was in tatters, and that his actions had caused him to make many enemies.

Eugene reached in his inside jacket pocket and removed a tattered envelope.

Eugene, Otha Lee;

Hopefully this letter finds you in God's gracious care.

Everything is moving on my end. I have in my time here in Dallas had the pleasure of making some very important enemies (smile). But that's neither here nor there.

What I need for you to know is that I leave behind two sons. One is there in Detroit with you, and the other is here with me. You do not have to worry about them financially, as I have made stipends for them both to be well taken care of.

I am writing you both merely to tell you that I love you, and I'm sorry that I brought you into this lifestyle. My hope is that you simply keep an eye on both of them.

My junior Julius will be looked after by Charlie Boy, and I want you guys to get to know him as well.

Devon, on the other hand, will be a different story. I know from experience that he will undoubtedly harbor anger, not only for me, but for his little brother as well. I pray that you don't let that happen. I need for them to share the same love that we as brothers shared when we were kids.

What I did to Daddy was not only for Mama, but for us also. I have a lot of regrets, but the only thing I can say that I will never regret is killing that old bastard. He was a cancer on this family, and I've tried to be a father and brother to you all.

I may not be alive by the time you receive this letter, but promise me that you will look after my boys and teach them our ways.

Sincerely,
JG

Tears welled up in the corners of his eyes as he thought of the lean years after Julius had murdered their father. They had been put into an orphanage, and Julius had been sent to the Arkansas Negro Boys Industrial School.

The State of Arkansas had sympathized with a distraught Julius, and had only sentenced him to serve six months for their father's death. But by the time he was released, his younger brothers were deep inside the system. They had been sent to St. Raphael's Orphanage in Pine Bluffs, and it had proven to be a nightmare.

Julius searched high and low for his younger brothers and had found them at St. Raphael's. He crept inside late one night and gathered his brothers, and they all disappeared into the night. They hopped train after train until they'd reached Detroit, where Julius felt that they were far enough away from Arkansas so that no one would be looking for them. But in reality, no one was looking for them. They were three less mouths to feed in an already overpopulated system of runaways and left-behinds.

Eugene folded the letter and put it back into his pocket. He and Otha Lee had some making up to do in terms of their nephews. They had let Julius Sr. down in a major way, but they would redeem themselves.

Tomorrow would be a new day, and after the Mexican threat was eliminated, a new beginning.

******

The Meeting:

Julius and Devon walked into the hotel restaurant and confirmed their reservation with the maître d', who was a tight necked elderly white man with a slight British accent. He eyed the immaculately dressed young black men curiously, wondering what their line of business might be. He dismissed his meddlesome prying and showed the men to their table. It was a booth that sat in a dark corner of the restaurant. It left the Gage family exposed with their backs against the wall, and no means of escape in the event that things went awry.

Julius voiced his displeasure to the maître d', who immediately gave them a choice of a new location.

Devon and Julius chose a table near the center of the massive dining room, facing the door. Although it was in the center of the restaurant, it was tucked inconspicuously near a large column. The area was brightly lit, and the family could see in all directions with no blind spots.

Eugene, Otha Lee, Devon and Julius took their seats at the round table. The silence loomed heavily over the table of anxious men.

Julius reached down and felt for the duffel bag that his uncles had brought with them. A half million dollars was a lot of money to essentially be giving away. Julius didn't understand why they should have to pay just for peace of mind, but his uncles had silenced his query. "This is business, junior. Check your emotions at the door," Eugene had told him, and that's exactly what he had done.

Devon leaned in close to whisper, much like a child sharing a forbidden secret. "All I know is those muthafuckas had better not try no slick shit, 'cause I'm bustin' first and asking questions later," he said.

Otha Lee looked at the young man and shook his head. Devon was merciless and extremely efficient with his skills, but in his uncle's eyes, he didn't think clearly. "You just keep that trigger finger down, nephew. There should be no need for that."

Devon looked at his uncle, mystified. He couldn't believe his ears. One of the first lessons he'd ever learned from them was to never underestimate anyone, and to trust no one. He knew better than to argue with Otha Lee. It would only cause disharmony, and every man present needed to be on point.

Two burly Mexican men walked into the restaurant and surveyed the area cautiously. They were dressed from head to toe in expensive black suits, black shirts and black ties.

Julius laughed to himself. The men resembled CIA agents with the exception of the black shirts. They even wore the signature earpieces.

One of the men disappeared outside, and reappeared moments later with the Barrera brothers in tow.

The Gage clan stood to greet the Mexicans, but they were waved down by Mike Barrera. "That won't be necessary, gentlemen. We'll keep this as brief and as informal as possible," he said.

Devon sniffed disdainfully. His patience was wearing thin. He had grown very protective of his younger brother, and any sign of a threat would not be tolerated.

Flaco and Devon locked eyes. "Is there something wrong, *pendejo*?" Flaco asked.

Devon opened his mouth to speak, but he could feel his uncle's hand on his knee, applying pressure. "Nah, we're good, playboy," he said instead, and shrugged the *pendejo* comment off.

Eugene smirked at Flaco, knowing full well that Devon would love to spill his blood. Eugene was proud of Devon. He was every father's dream. He was a quick study, and excelled in everything he tried. His only wish was that Devon and Julius' father could have been there to see his sons.

"Let's get down to business, shall we? I believe that you have money for us, no?" Mike said, pulling a chair out to seat himself.

Flaco took the cue and sat down beside his brother.

Otha Lee nodded to Julius, who in turn slid the duffel bag to Flaco underneath the table.

"Do I need to count this?" Flaco asked. He eyed Julius as if he wanted to rip him apart.

Julius angrily glared back at Flaco. It was bad enough that they were demanding money, but the fact that Flaco had the audacity to question his integrity made Julius' blood boil. "You can do whatever you want to do, but it's all there. Have I ever played with your fucking money, Flaco?" Julius asked.

Mike chimed in cheerfully, trying desperately to

diffuse the situation before things got out of hand. "This should just about cover the loss of our nephew and the return of your soon to be mother-in-law." He looked up at one of his henchmen and nodded. "Tito, go and retrieve Mrs. Gray," he ordered him. "Gentlemen, let us toast to new beginnings," he said, and raised his glass, but no one else present made a move.

Flaco silently fumed. How dare his brother make his nephew's death a business deal? If things went according to *his* plan, his family would be the only ones to walk out of the Adolphus Hotel alive.

Julius anxiously looked towards the door. He expected Mrs. Gray to walk into the restaurant, shaken and beaten.

Moments later she appeared, and Julius' breath caught in his throat. She was absolutely gorgeous, and looked to be in perfect health; almost glowing. Her beauty was radiant; she glowed with the light of a woman that carried a beautiful secret. She wore a long, tight fitting but flowing white dress that seemed to accentuate every curve in her body. Her caramel colored skin shimmered from the glitter in her lotion, and she sashayed towards the table with a confident swagger.

As she approached, Julius stood and they embraced. "Are you okay, Veronica?" he asked.

"I'm fine, honey. Don't I look okay?"

"You look amazing! It's just that... well... the pictures that we received..." Julius began, letting his words trail off.

"I'm fine," Veronica said with down turned eyes.

Julius had obviously struck a nerve, but he decided against pressing the issue further. He was bewildered by her glow, but also relieved to see her in good health.

Eugene eyed the older woman curiously. His nephew had told him of her situation, but he had neglected to tell him how beautiful she was. "So, this should conclude our business, am I correct, gentlemen? I have your complete assurance that my nephews will go unharmed?" Eugene asked.

Flaco was mute. His attention was fixed on Devon. The young black man irritated him. His brash personality grated Flaco's nerves. His jaws tensed, and he sprang from his seat with his pistol in hand, aimed at Devon. "Do you think that you're a gangster, *panzòn*?" he asked.

The two goons also drew their weapons.

"Listen, Flaco. Let's not do anything we'll regret, *mi hermano*!" Mike pleaded.

"Hold up Mike you ain't gotta say shit. Your pussy ass brother already tried to have my mother killed. You overstepped your bounds fuckboy." Julius exclaimed.

"Save it, Mikey! These *pinché miates* are going to pay for killing my nephew! And as for your mother Julius chinge' tu madre' puto!!" Flaco screamed.

Flaco's tirade drew the attention of nearby patrons, who upon seeing the guns began to panic and scream.

In the distance the sound of shattering glass could

be heard as the biggest Mexican guard, Gordo slumped to the ground with thick, gooey blood oozing from his temple.

Another bullet struck the second guard, Tito's hand, causing him to drop his weapon and drop to the floor in pain. His scream of agony drew Flaco's attention, and he turned to see both of the body guards sprawled out on the floor. One was dead, and the other one was holding his exploded hand and squirming in pain.

The instant Flaco turned his head to see what was going on, all of the Gage men drew their weapons.

Mike sat in a shocked daze, unable to move.

Restaurant patrons began stampeding out of the restaurant in hysterics.

Otha Lee took aim across the table with his .357 and let his Magnum bark in Mike's direction. The slug entered the older Mexican man's eye and exited the back of his head, spraying blood and brain matter across the table behind him.

Veronica's scream and the thunderous sound of the .357 cannon drew Flaco's attention back to the table. He turned to see his only brother slumped in his chair. Mike's blood seeped onto the milky white table cloth, dying it a dull crimson red. In a bewildered daze, Flaco dropped his pistol and knelt down next to his brother.

Devon took aim at Flaco, but before he could get a shot off, the side of Flaco's body exploded in a shower of red.

Veronica screamed again. The sight of her lover collapsing was too much for her to bear. She didn't know where the mysterious shots were coming from, but she didn't want to wait to find out.

The four Gage men looked at one another in confusion. None of them had delivered the shots, and nobody else in their family was at the meeting.

******

Across the street from the Adolphus Hotel on the roof of the Neiman Marcus building, Shayla caressed the trigger of her AR15 gently. She had taken out the limousine driver and his partner first. They seemed to be planning something sinister as they sat in the limousine. *Two shots, two kills, Devon would be proud*, she thought. Shayla peered through the scope of her assault rifle, scanning the restaurant for any further signs of danger. There were none.

As she settled her scope on Devon's table, she smirked as her man and his family tried to figure out who their guardian angel was. Devon had no idea that Shayla had disobeyed his orders for her to go to Jamaica with Angelica and Naje'. She couldn't leave his safety to chance, so she'd come to Dallas against his wishes.

Sirens in the distance pulled Shayla from her daydream. Devon must've heard the sirens too, because he, Julius and Angelica's mother scrambled frantically for the kitchen, as two older black men who she figured had to be their uncles, picked up a duffel bag and strolled casually towards the front door.

Shayla placed her assault rifle in its case and headed towards the fire escape where her car waited below.

******

Julius, Devon and Veronica burst through the double doors leading to the kitchen. They scrambled frantically between stainless steel food prep tables, deep fryers and stoves, nervously making their way towards the rear exit.

Devon heard the swinging doors crash open behind him and instinctively raised his pistol and took aim. He fired just as Tito raised his pistol in his direction. Devon's bullet struck the Mexican soldier in his chest.

The .45 caliber bullet stopped him in his tracks, knocked him backwards and twisted his body viciously. "Ahh! *Pinché pendejo!*" Tito shrieked.

Julius stopped running as pandemonium broke out in the kitchen. Waiters dropped trays on the floor and the chefs abandoned their prized dishes as they all made a mad dash for safety.

In the melee, Tito's gun was kicked from his hand. He lay on the floor, thrashing in pain. Julius walked back to where the man lay, aimed his 9mm and pumped two slugs into his forehead. Tito's body went limp as brain and blood matter oozed from the gaping hole at the back of his head.

"Ju come on, nigga! We gotta go!" Devon screamed.

Julius seemed to not hear his brother calling his name.

Veronica stood there, dumbstruck. She had heard stories of Julius' ruthlessness, but she only knew the Julius that loved her daughter. She didn't know this side of him and it frightened her.

"Julius! Julius, let's go, my nigga!" Devon shouted again.

Julius joined Devon and Veronica as they ran towards the exit. In the distance police sirens wailed. Devon clutched Veronica's hand and burst through the back door, followed closely by Julius. The trio quickly scurried down the alley towards Main Street, with Devon nearly dragging Veronica. The commotion was on Commerce Street behind them, so they anxiously made their way in the opposite direction.

"You need to slow the fuck down, bro. You're gonna draw heat moving so fast," Julius warned.

As if in agreement, Devon slowed to a normal pace. "Yo, did you see which way Unc n'em went?" he asked.

"Nah, man. But we need to get somewhere safe and *then* worry about them. I'm sure that they know what they're doing."

Devon was about to respond when the sound of an engine roaring towards them drew their attention. They turned to see high-beam headlights speeding in their direction.

Julius raised his pistol to fire but, Devon grabbed his arm and said, "Put that shit away, fool! You're talking about me drawing heat?"

"What the fuck are you doing, my nig? I'm not going back to jail. Bust first and ask questions later, remember?" Julius said sarcastically.

Devon smirked. He knew his little brother meant every word. "Yeah, I understand that, but look. That car doesn't have flashers or sirens. Whoever it is must be a civilian, probably running from the restaurant too."

The closer the headlights got to them, the brighter they seemed. The car then came to a screeching halt only a couple of feet from where they stood.

Julius and Devon squinted futilely against the blinding lights as Veronica cowered behind the young men, trembling in fear. The lights went off, and Julius inched back closer to Veronica to protect her. It was pitch black in the alley, except for the over-head lights that bounced lazily off of the slick, wet asphalt.

Shayla jumped out of the car, smiling broadly. "Y'all gonna stand there looking all scared and shit, or are y'all gonna get in the car so that we can get the fuck out of here?" she teased. She closed the door of the white Mercedes Benz and ran to her man.

Devon couldn't believe his eyes. He had left her in Florida, thinking that she was headed to Jamaica with Angelica and Najé. He gave her a bear hug. He was beyond grateful that she was safe. He kissed her deeply and looked into her eyes. "What the fuck are you doing here, Shayla? I thought I told you to get on the plane with Najé and Angelica?" he scolded.

"I know what you said, baby, but I also made you a promise a long time ago. I meant it when I told you that I would always have your back. It took me a very long time to get you to love me as your woman, and I won't lose that because you wanna go and get killed. Now, let's go, baby. You can fuss at me later.

Epilogue

Four Years Later

The Mexican woman and the ex-detective sat far enough away so that they could watch the family and still remain unnoticed.

All of Sweeney's years on the force had come in handy since connecting with Ms. Barrera. She had bonded him out of jail, put money in his pocket and promised to make him wealthy beyond his wildest dreams under one condition: that he help her kill Julius and Devon Gage and all that they hold dear.

******

Sweeney had awoken in a hospital bed. His eyes

burned from the bright overhead fluorescent lights, and his mouth was beyond dry. He tried unsuccessfully to swallow, and when he did it felt as though he was swallowing sand. He tried to lift his hands to wipe the sleep from his eyes, but he was shackled to a hospital bed.

He looked towards the door and squinted, trying desperately to grab the attention of a passing nurse or doctor, but his eyes met a closed door.

He looked to his left and noticed a small framed Mexican woman with greying hair seated next to his bed. Her head was bowed as if in prayer. Between her praying hands dangled a gold and diamond encrusted rosary. He shifted to focus, and an insurmountable pain surged through his body. He winced and groaned in pain. The sound barely escaped his lips and it was nearly inaudible, but it was loud enough to draw the woman from prayer.

"Thank God you are finally awake!" she said.

Sweeney looked at the woman. Her eyes were hollow, as though she'd lived through too much pain. "I'm sorry," his voice cracked. "Do I know you?"

"No, but I know you, or rather I know *of* you. I also know that we have a common enemy. Does the name 'Gage' ring a bell?" she said with a smile.

As Sweeney struggled against his restraints, the handcuffs clanged against the metal railings of the hospital bed.

"Relax. I am not here to harm you," The woman said, still smiling. "I believe that we can help one another."

"And just how can you help me, lady? Maybe you haven't noticed, but I'm shackled to a hospital bed," he said sarcastically.

"My friend, your bond has been posted for quite some time now. The restraints can be removed at any time. All I need is your word that you'll help me eliminate the Gage brothers and everything that they love, and you are a free man."

"And if I refuse?" he asked.

"I prefer to start with the positive, Detective Sweeney. If you do choose to help me, the world is your oyster and I will make you a very rich man. But if you refuse to help me, I will simply have your bond revoked, remove my lawyers from your case and walk away. It is of no consequence to me if you choose to spend the rest of your life in prison. There are plenty of *soldados* that would love to make $200,000 per hit." She watched as Sweeney's eyes lit up with greed.

"And how many hits are we talking, lady?"

"As many as it takes to eliminate even the faintest whisper of the Gage name," She said with a smirk, knowing full well that she had his attention. She pressed on. "I have no reason to lie to you. My money is limitless. For more than a year I have been sitting by your bedside praying that you would awaken and join me, and now that you are awake you have doubts?"

Sweeney's head was spinning. *What the fuck is she talking about?* he wondered. "What the fuck do you mean by more than a year?"

"I mean that you have been in a coma for more than a year," she pointedly stated.

It was then that he realized that he'd lost it all. He didn't have anything. His apartment and all of his belongings would surely be gone by now. His career was gone, and the Department would have in all certainty seized all of his assets, considering that they had evidence of corruption.

******

That conversation had been almost four years earlier, and Carmelita had held true to her promise. They had yet to harm a hair on the Gages' heads, yet she paid Sweeney $5000 a week faithfully. She told him to be patient and get well, and that's exactly what he had done.

Ms. Barrera had become his responsibility, so much so that some of her bodyguards were jealous, referring to Sweeney as a "glorified errand boy". She was immensely loyal, and he tried everything in his power to return that loyalty. The feeling was new to him. Sweeney had never been loyal to anything or anyone his entire life, but this was different. He was essentially being paid for his friendship.

And now here they were, sitting in a dark sedan across from a crowded park, watching the Gage boys enjoys family time with their children. It had taken them a while, but they'd finally tracked them down to the suburban neighborhood of Buckhead, in Atlanta, Georgia.

Sweeney screwed the silencer onto the barrel of his 9mm pistol and put it in the waistband of his camel colored linen slacks.

"Don't do anything until I give you the green light, *mi amor*. Do you understand?" Ms. Barrera asked.

"Yes, I understand, my dear."

Sweeney stepped out of the sedan, walked to the passenger's side and opened the door for the Carmelita. She held his hand tightly, as if they were an old, love struck couple.

The two strolled along the sidewalk holding hands, and pretended to look at several houses with for sale signs on plush, green lawns. When they were adjacent to the family, they crossed the street, keeping a close eye on Julius and Devon Gage.

Sweeney and Ms. Barrera sat down on a bench not twenty feet from where the family played with their children.

Three children played near the playground, while their young parents looked on. There were numerous children on the playground, but these three seemed to be content with playing amongst each other.

The little boy and little girl looked very close in age, while the third child, a boy, seemed to be slightly younger.

Sweeney eyed the children curiously. He had no conscience, so murdering children was not beneath him. The three children would die first, then the women, and then the Gage boys. He wanted them to know the ultimate pain before they died. He giggled at the thought of letting them live just long enough to bury their loved ones, and know that it was their lifestyle and choices that had caused their family's demise. His trigger finger twitched with anticipation, and he subconsciously squeezed Ms. Barrera's frail hand.

"Aye-e-e, *chigado*! Is there something wrong?" she asked.

He looked at her with sad, wanting eyes, wishing that she would free him to do her bidding. He wanted and needed for them to experience as much emotional pain as possible.

"In due time, my love. Be patient." she said in an effort to soothe his blood lust.

******

Angelica rested her head in Julius' lap and stared into a brooding Atlanta sky while he played with her hair and caressed her cheek gently. "What's wrong, baby? Looks like you have something on your mind," she said.

He smiled at her, and then looked out onto the playground. Their son was a mini version of him, and it made him think about his father. He could still remember so much from his young years, and lately the death of his Aunt Pearl in the parking lot of the Red Door Motel had been playing over and over again in his head. "I'm straight. I just look at the baby, and it makes me think about my daddy. It makes me wonder if I'll be here for my son, or be killed in these streets," he said reflectively.

He was talking *at* Angelica instead of *to* her, but she understood his concern. "You'll be around forever, baby. You're too stubborn and mean to die," she said.

They both laughed at the thought.

Julius loved Angelica and he loved his son, Julius Gage III, or Trey as they affectionately called him. He was the apple of his parents' eyes. He was somewhat rambunctious, which caused them to be just a tad bit overprotective. But after the life that they had lived, it was a necessary evil.

Angelica watched, as Trey tossed the big red ball between him, Julianna and AJ. She understood Julius' concern, but she was thankful for the type of father that he had turned out to be. He had given up the hustling lifestyle as promised, and had made good on his word of going to college. At times she found it overwhelming, juggling her last year in college, being a full time mom and planning a wedding, but she was handling it the best way possible.

Having Devon, Shayla and their daughter, Julianna there with them made things a little easier, but it was a daily challenge just the same.

Angelica loved Julianna. She and Trey were only two months apart, and they were as close as twins; almost inseparable. Najé and Veronica called them the "Bobsy Twins" because where there was one, the other was close by. Although Julianna was a mere two months Trey's senior, she felt it necessary to protect her little cousin, and that usually meant going against anyone and anything.

Najé and Veronica sat on a nearby bench conversing about their children and grandchildren.

Out of the corner of her eye, Najé noticed Trey walking toward an elderly couple sitting on a park bench near the playground. Her maternal instincts were in overdrive, especially considering the events that had transpired over the course of the last few years.

She looked around the playground searching for any sign of alarm from either Julius or Angelica and saw them lying on a plush, blue and white checkered blanket. They were watching Treys' every move, so there was obviously no need for her to be alarmed.

Najé heard Veronica talking, but she wasn't listening. She was captivated by the elderly couple that Trey had now made his way over to. She watched as the elderly Spanish woman knelt in front of Trey to give him the ball that had made its way to their location. Something in the eyes of the man that was with the woman struck her as familiar.

"What are you staring at, Ma?" Devon asked her. He and Shayla had walked up behind the two women.

"Just watching your nephew talk this woman's ear off."

"You know that boy is a social butterfly. He'll talk to the wind if he thinks that it'll talk back."

They all laughed because it was true.

At five years old he was advanced beyond his years. The conversations that Najé had with her grandson sounded more like two adults rather than an adult and a five year old child. She sometimes felt as if his grandfather had been reincarnated as her grandson, because he had an old soul.

******

Ms. Barrera knelt down in front of the little boy and handed him his shiny red ball. "Hello, *mijo*. What is your name?" she asked.

"My name is Julius, but everybody calls me Trey. What does *mijo* mean?"

"*Mijo* means baby boy in Spanish, little one."

"Oh, well I'm not a baby, I'm a big boy!" Trey exclaimed.

"That you are, my love. Is that your family over there?" she asked, motioning towards Julius and

Angelica.

"Uh huh. That's my mommy, and my daddy, and my two nanas, and my Uncle Devon, and Auntie Shay, and my cousin Julianna, and my Uncle AJ," he said all in one breath.

"He's your uncle? He's a little young to be your uncle isn't he?" Ms. Barrera asked inquisitively.

"That's my —"

Before he could finish his sentence, Julianna was pulling at his hand. "Trey, you know we're not supposed to talk to strangers. You're gonna get in trouble," she said in her small but bossy voice.

"I know that, Anna! Da-a-a-ang!"

Devon walked over to them, shaking his head. His daughter and nephew were two of a kind. He smiled to himself and thought, *Those kids can make friends with a tree stump!* "I'm sorry, ma'am. Are they bothering you?" he asked.

"No, no, not at all. They are absolutely adorable!" she said, trying to muster as much broken English as possible. "He," she began, pointing to Trey, "Says that the little one is his uncle. I guess he meant cousin?"

"Who, AJ? He is his uncle. He's his grandmother's son. She's a late bloomer," Devon said jokingly.

Ms. Barrera studied the little boy carefully. He reminded her of Sleepy when he was that age.

Devon noticed her staring at AJ with tears welling in her eyes. "Are you okay, ma'am?" he asked.

"I'm fine. He just reminds me of someone very dear to me who I lost some years back."

"I'm sorry to hear that. Well, you and your husband have a nice day. Come on, kids. Why don't we leave these nice people alone. Say goodbye.

"By-y-y-ye!" both children said in sing-song unison.

Devon looked at the elderly couple and smiled, only to notice the older man eyeing him as if he'd eaten the big piece of chicken at the dinner table. He gathered the children and made his way back to where his family was waiting.

"What's wrong, bro? You got that funny look in your eyes," Julius said.

"I'm straight. That lady over there just kinda fucked my head up the way she was looking at AJ. And then her husband was looking at me like he wanted to kill a nigga."

"He's probably one of these Georgia rednecks that don't like black people, mane. Fuck him!" Julius exclaimed loudly.

"Nah, it's more than that. It's like I swear I've seen that dude somewhere or something."

The hair on the back of Najé's neck stood up. "Me too, Devon. He looks really familiar. Something about him isn't right," she said.

Sweeney noticed the entire family staring in his direction and talking amongst each other, and it made him uncomfortable. He stood up and adjusted the pistol in his waistband. "It's now or never, Ms. B. let me do them all right here, right now!" he exclaimed.

"Not yet. Let them wonder, *mi amor*. Just a few more moments."

Trey's young voice drew everyone's attention. "Nana, AJ is going to the water!" he whined.

Veronica stood and peered across the playground, trying to spot AJ. Her beloved only son headed towards a deep creek that rushed wildly and crashed against the large rocks at the bottom of the hill. Her heart sank, "AJ!" she screamed, but he didn't seem to hear her.

AJ was chasing the red ball that he and his playmates had found so much amusement in only moments earlier. His tiny legs would carry him close to the ball, only to have his foot kick it just out of his reach before he could get to it.

"*AJ!*" Veronica screamed again, but AJ continued meandering toward the slope of the hill that led downward toward the brook.

"Mama, go get him!" Angelica screamed frantically. She could see her little brother disappearing into the horizon of the now graying sky. The sun had begun to set, and it painted the sky depressing hues of oranges and grays.

Moving hastily in his direction, Veronica yelled one last time. "AJ! Antonio Barrera Jr., I know you hear me calling you! Come away from that water!" she shouted.

"Ball, Mommy!" AJ yelled back.

"I know you want your ball, honey bunny, but we have to go now, okay?"

******

A look of terror washed over Ms. Barrera's face. She felt a sinking feeling in the pit of her stomach. That was the reason the little boy reminded her so much of Sleepy. He was Flaco's son, who was badly wounded from the shooting at the Adolphus hotel. He had been in a near vegetative state for months afterward, and she had stayed by his side, shuffling between caring for him and caring for Sweeney. He hadn't faired quite as well as Sweeney, but he was still alive nevertheless. He had no clue whatsoever that he was a father. Maybe... just maybe knowing that he had a son would bring him back to the Flaco that she had always loved. "I am ready to leave, *mi amor*," she said to Sweeney.

"But—" Sweeney began.

"Now, Sweeney!" she said more firmly. "I have something better than death in store for these *pinché miates*, and with what I have in mind, they will crave death!" Ms. Barrera said firmly as she hurriedly rushed Sweeney towards their waiting sedan.

******

Devon racked his brain trying to remember where he had met the man before. He never forgot a face; a name yes, but never a face. He scanned his mental rolodex trying to place the man.

As the dark sedan passed Devon's car, Sweeney menacingly peered out of the driver's side window at the Gage family.

Julius locked eyes with the man as he sped away. "Man, that's why he didn't look right, y'all. That's that crooked muthafucka, Detective Sweeney!" he yelled.

Sneak Preview
Of The Upcoming Novel

Tainted